Happy

Spirits of the Past: Book One

The Black Lion

Richard B Gough

The Black Lion, Spirits of the Past: Book One

ISBN: 9781720258056

www.richardbgough.com

The Black Lion

The Black Lion

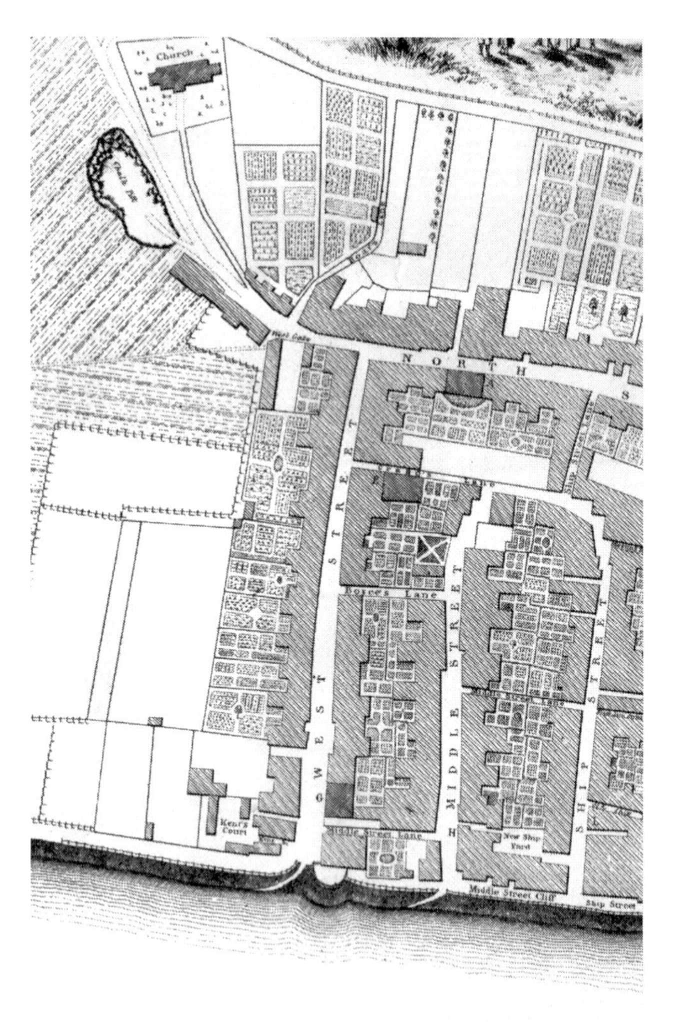

A very fine Sand dry

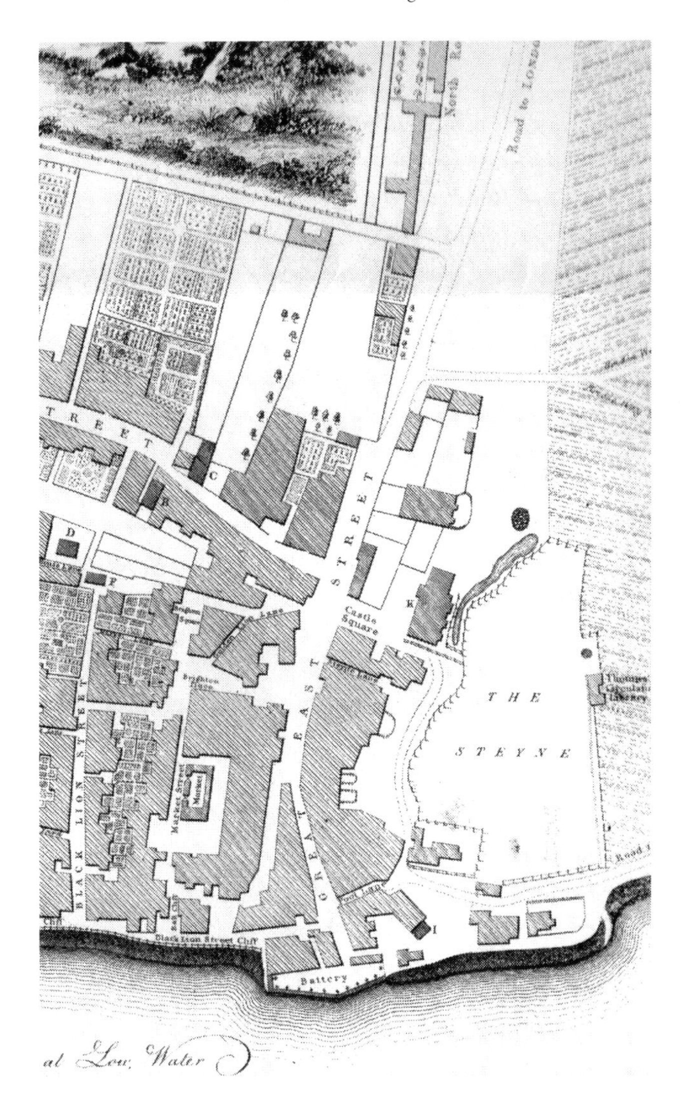
Road to LONDON
North
STREET
STREET
Castle Square
EAST STREET
GREAT
THE
STEYNE
BLACK LION STREET
Market
Market Street
Black Lion Street Cliff
Battery
at Low Water

Special Thanks to

My husband Michael for his ongoing support and constructive feedback during the writing and reviewing process. It really meant a lot to me.

My editor Jayne Raven (pen name Charlie Raven) for giving 'The Black Lion' a final polish. I'm so pleased I found you! For more info, please visit her website www.ravenswritingdesk.uk

My friends and authors:

Rohase Piercy for recommending Jayne 'Charlie' Raven. For further info visit their website: www.theravensbunker.com

Pete Blakey-Novis for being an early reader.

Shani Struthers for her generous support.

Vee McGivney for her useful preliminary advice.

My beta readers Angi, Chris, Doris, John and Simone for reviewing the book.

Bridget Whelan and Jill Vigus for their workshop at the Regency Town House in Hove, back in 2018, which inspired me to write this book.

Author and historian Judy Middleton for featuring the wonderful story about the Legend of St Ann's Well on her website. The story is recounted in full on hovehistory.blog.com

The Society of Print Collectors who kindly gave me permission to use the map of Brighthelmstone.

The Keep, the libraries, and the internet for keeping records of historic Brighthelmstone, Britain and Europe which were essential to write Deryk's story.

Encyclopaedia Brittanica, Foxe's Book of Martyrs, The Lewes Bonfire Society, The Royal Pavilion catalogue and free online encyclopaedia Wikipedia.

In the course of my research, I consulted many different sources and was inspired by the work of many different authors. Any failure on my part to attribute quotations, ideas or research correctly is not intentional and will be corrected at the earliest opportunity.

Regarding the unknown man featured on the front cover, back in December 2018 I met up with my friend Carolyn in Black Lion Lane to take some photos for the book. Suddenly a man turned into the lane and we stopped talking. An eerie silence followed whilst he started walking towards us. He passed us outside Black Lion Cottage and apologised for photobombing my picture. After I came home, streaming the pictures on my phone, I found out I captured the man the precise moment he stepped into the lane.

Finally I would like to thank *you* and I hope you enjoy reading this book as much as I enjoyed writing it.

"The mystery of love is greater than the mystery of death."

Oscar Wilde

Deryk

It was the year of Our Lord 1555, the Twenty-Second of July, and I was standing in deep thought at the bottom of the stone steps, looking up towards the light beyond. I was awaiting my final doom. I stood in the vaults below the street, hemmed in by limestone walls set with ancient candle brackets every few feet. For centuries, rain had seeped through the mouldy cracks between the beige and blue-grey stones and the air smelt musty.

Outside the Star Inn, people had gathered to watch the preparations being made for an auto-da-fé. Slowly, barefooted, I started climbing the worn steps, gazing at the rays of the bright sun in the sky above me. When I reached the top, Sheriff Cage was waiting for me to fulfil the Bishop's verdict: for I had opposed the Queen's religious changes and had refused to recant and convert to Catholicism.

This would be my final day on earth. Approaching the Star Inn, I saw a crowd gathered around a stake, stacked high with straw bales, which had been erected in the middle of the road. With a dreadful irony, a barrel had been placed in front of it, a mockery of my profession as a brewer. I was sure the Sheriff smirked when he kneeled down in front of it, bowing his head and closing his eyes.

After he had said his prayer, he stood up and said to me, "Now, Deryk Carver, before you sacrifice your body, you will need to strip off all your clothes."
Within a minute I stood stark naked in front of strangers, displaying my black-haired body. The Sheriff showed the crowd my prayer book, the Luther Bible, then threw it into the barrel, and addressed me: "Deryk Carver, do you have anything to say?"
Instinctively I bent and removed the book and threw it among the people, hoping someone would catch it to keep it safe.
Instantly the Sheriff shouted to the mob: "In the name of the Queen, on pain of death, put the book back into the barrel!"
The crowd fell quiet. People glanced around without a single word: it looked as if the book had mysteriously disappeared. Despite the loss of the book, the Sheriff commanded me to step into the barrel, hastily tying my hands and feet tightly to the stake before he lit the torch and set light to the wood beneath. There was not much time left.
Quickly, looking out upon the bystanders, I started to speak. "Dear brothers and sisters, naked I came from my mother's womb, and naked I shall return!"
The people murmured appreciatively and many of them applauded my words whilst the flames were licking the crackling wood. The smell of the smoke was deep and

oaky, and the heat of the fire was intense.
Deep in my heart I was frightened, but I managed to continue my speech. "Today I have come to spill my blood in the name of true religion. For decades during the reigns of our sovereign lords Henry VIII and Edward VI many people read and preached from the very same book as I did, not only here in Lewes, but in all the places in the realm of England - until Queen Mary ascended the throne. Then at once it was forbidden!"
The spectators cheered and raised their arms to show their support. I looked around, content to see that so many people agreed with me. "Last year they arrested me on All-Hallows-Eve, and ten days ago, Bishop Bonner asked me to recant, to which I answered: 'Over my dead body.' He said I would burn in hell and hence I am here today in front of you, condemned to die.
Some people say our bodies are strong, but I believe our spirits are stronger."
The orange flames reached higher, the heat turning my skin red. My voice sounded high pitched when I next managed to speak: "Please do not forsake my children, my brewery, and all I ever had. I fear this is the end and I vow to ask forgiveness for all our sins. I commend my spirit to rejoice in You, O Lord. Please, receive my spirit!"
I sprang up as my body became one with the inferno. My spirit rose with the black smoke and burning embers, high above the hills of Lewes, gazing down at the streets,

hoping this town would always remember my name.
That summer afternoon my soul floated through the air, light as a feather, listening to the sounds of the birds around me, but then the sky became empty. The birds disappeared, and I realised I was missing my dearest friend. I looked for him everywhere, behind the sun and behind the clouds, but I couldn't find him. With a forlorn feeling I continued my journey through the sky, until I saw clouds which looked like steps leading up to the sky. Would there be a man waiting for me at the entrance of the large black and gold gates in the clouds? Would he open his book and look up my name, then tell me those not fit to enter heaven would be denied entrance at the gates, and their spirit would descend into hell?
It is believed this is the final destiny of those who have not been found worthy, and where they will be eternally punished for their sins.
Suddenly, I heard a voice whispering from the sky: "You are denied entrance. Your soul should be damned, just as your body has been burned, but I will lay a last commandment upon you: to return and live amongst the undead until, perhaps, one day, you can find the soul of the friend you had to leave behind. And then your souls will rise together and return to these gates, and I will reconsider. You are denied entrance, for now.'
I was astounded. Saint Peter had given me a hope of redeeming myself from hell. Instead I would be living as

a spirit, invisible to the living, until my change came. I looked down and it seemed to me that I saw somebody kneeling at the smouldering stake in the middle of the road. In his hand he held a black rose, which he placed at the foot of the stake. He looked up at the sky and in my vision, I saw the sun reflecting in his eyes. Unmistakably, it was he, my dearest friend: but whether in reality or whether our souls had connected in a dream, I did not know. In my mind I said to him: 'Wait for me. One day I will return and I will find you.'

For Sale

Matt, born and bred in Brighton, completed the fellowship route of the Chartered Institute of Legal Executives in his early twenties and became a successful solicitor at Clark and Mitchell Associates. Brighton, a busy hub attracting both local visitors and people from all over the world, was once a fishing village. It became a well-known English seaside resort. It's about an hour south of London by train, with a broad pebble beach, a beautiful Victorian pier, and iconic Regency-era buildings.

A decade after Matt had started working for the successful law firm at Moore House, a newly built office had been acquired, a stone's throw away from Brighton station.

Matt would miss this part of the old town, especially because his childhood friend grew up in Black Lion Cottage, just around the corner from the office. It was part of a terrace of sixteenth century cottages situated in a very narrow passageway between two pubs, The Black Lion and The Cricketers. He had stayed there a couple of times and Matt had never forgotten how it felt in the cottage, the sense of

history being alive around him.
Matt emptied out his drawers, picked up his Stonewall Diversity award, wrapped it in brown paper, and carefully placed it in the removal box, preparing himself for the move.

All staff members had decided to meet up for drinks in the pub next door, The Black Lion. Matt and his colleague Kate, a Legal Secretary, entered the pub and headed straight to the bar to order their drinks. Kate was a bit of a chatterbox but they had got on really well from the first moment they met, probably because he was more of a quiet person.
"Matt, I'm so going to miss Moore House, it's so close to the seafront, isn't it?"
"I'm going to miss it too, Kate. But on a positive note, the new office is close to the North Laine and Queen's Road. Just think of all the coffee places and shops we can explore together on our lunch breaks. And if you'd like, you can still go down to the pier. It's only a ten minute walk."
"That's true, but you know what I'm like, I like to have things on my doorstep." Abruptly she changed the subject. "Something just sprung to my mind, I completely forgot to tell you. Earlier today I was speaking to Sue, our bookkeeper, and when I asked whether she knew anything about the history of our

office she told me Moore House used to be called The Brewery Shades."
"The Brewery Shades?"
"Well, Sue has been living here for over sixty years, she's part of the furniture, and she knows a lot." Kate explained. "Sue has witnessed much of Black Lion Street being redeveloped over time and nowadays The Black Lion pub exists at 14 Black Lion Street. She said the former brewery used to stand next to the pub before the brewery and inn were demolished."
"So we've been working where the brewery once stood. Did Sue happen to tell you when the pub was built?"
"That's funny, I asked her the same question. I thought it was several hundreds of years old, but guess what? The original Black Lion brewery and inn was demolished in the 1960s and rebuilt early 1970s."
"Really? I didn't know that. It looks very old. I always liked the old town, you can feel the history coming to life when you walk through the streets. Those memories of history seem to have imprinted themselves onto the atmosphere."
"Talking about history, let me show you something!" Kate opened her handbag. "Sue gave me this copy of today's paper - it's got two photos of The Brewery

Shades - the *Argus* often features local history pieces - and I'm sure you'll be interested to see them. Here, look! The first one is Black Lion Street circa 1900. At the right you can just see the edge of The Cricketers pub; next to it is the corner of the brewery that was rebuilt in 1974 as The Black Lion pub. At the far end of the brewery building is The Brewery Shades, it's the building with the two gables. The second picture was taken in the mid 1960s. Then it was called Framlins Brewery and it's to the right of that. The brewery buildings survived until May 1969 before they were demolished but, the cottages behind the wall of the brewery remained untouched."

"That all sounds very mysterious and it sounds like the pub must have been moved. Well, they've done a great job, and spookily it looks very much like the original."

"The Cricketers next door is still the original building, and according to their staff the pub is haunted. My cousin Pat, who works at the bar, has seen bottles and glasses falling off the shelves, doors suddenly slam shut. One evening she even heard footsteps climbing the stairs. On several occasions a pale man with a beard, wearing a long black cloak, was spotted in the little narrow lane which runs between the two pubs. It's called Black Lion Lane."

Suddenly a strange feeling came over Matt.
"Sorry to change the subject, but do you happen to know whether the pub has always been called The Black Lion?"
"Interestingly, for most of the 1970s, the pub was called The Deryk Carver but a decade later it seemed to have reverted to The Black Lion, and nobody knows why."
"How odd. So, who was Deryk Carver?" Matt took a sip of his glass of red wine.
"He used to run The Black Lion brewery and inn."
"So he lived before it was called The Brewery Shades?"
"Oh yes, he lived well before that. He lived in the sixteenth century. I actually looked him up on Wikipedia, after Sue showed me these photos. He's a really interesting character. Did you know he was one of the first brewers to introduce beer here? People mainly used to drink ale in those days. Apparently, the brewery was quite big. It had a cellar, a freshwater well, and three old tenements with dormer windows. Deryk was originally from Belgium and you can imagine the beer he brewed was heady and became very popular. But, this is the bit of the story that really caught my imagination; his life was cut short very tragically. His views didn't go down well with the religious leaders of the time.

He was arrested after reading from a forbidden book in front of guests in his pub, put in prison in London, and finally burned § at the stake in Lewes. Carver's ghost is said to haunt the cellars of the pub, especially on 31st October. Hallowe'en is the anniversary of his arrest."
Matt felt pity for the man. "It's horrific what they did to him. His spirit must have struggled to find peace when he was burned. But suppose if I was a ghost, wouldn't I do the same thing, frightening the hell out of people to have a little bit of fun?" He sighed and looked at the clock on the wall. "Oh gosh, is it that time already? Kate, it was lovely to see you, but I'm afraid I've got to dash."
"Likewise, it's been good to see you too. Have you got any plans for the weekend? Off to the clubs again?"
"Tonight I'm meeting my friends at Legends and we'll probably end up in one of the sleazy clubs. What are your plans?"
"I'm going to spend the whole weekend in bed with Julie watching films, drinking beer, eating pizzas and ...," Kate's eyes glistened as she took a gulp of beer. "Oh, Matt, before you go, did you know that one of The Black Lion cottages around the corner is up for sale?"
Matt's jaw dropped. "Up for sale? I used to play in

one of the cottages with a childhood friend who grew up there. Do you happen to know who I can contact?"
"No, but I saw it advertised in this newspaper. Here, have a look!" He flicked through the pages until his eyes caught a small advert with a picture of an old timber style cottage. He recognised it instantly.

Property for sale: a three bedroom grade II listed cottage of historic interest in central Brighton. Tucked away in one of Brighton's oldest twittens, this cottage is superbly situated in the heart of the Lanes. The row of cottages along Black Lion Lane, are reputedly the oldest houses in Brighton, dating back to the sixteenth century. This cottage is one of three in a row and is ideal as a 'buy-to-let' property. Close to Brighton mainline station with direct links to London. Viewing highly recommended. Guide price: POA. Please contact Craig on the number below.

"Thanks for this, Kate. Have a great weekend and I'll see you on Monday in our new office." He gave her a peck on her cheek.
"You too darling. Don't do anything I wouldn't do!" she said with a smile.
After leaving the pub Matt called the number.

“Good afternoon, Craig speaking.”
“Hi Craig, my name is Matt. I just saw your advert in the Argus and wondered if the cottage is still vacant?”
“We have a couple of cottages on sale at the moment. Which one did you see advertised?” Craig enquired.
“It’s Black Lion Cottage, I saw it in today’s edition?”
“Let me have a look for you on my computer. Ah, I’ve found it, yes, the cottage is still vacant.”
“Great. I wonder why the current owner is selling? It’s one of the oldest buildings in Brighton.”
“They’re selling due to private circumstances. There’s no chain. It will be a quick sale”.
Matt arranged to view the cottage straight away. As he waited for Craig outside, he studied the characterful three storey building compromising three terraced cottages. The upper storeys were bigger than the ground floor and overhung it, giving maximum width to the lane below.
A man holding a folder underneath his arm turned into the narrow lane and walked towards him, making eye-contact.“Hi, I’m Craig. You must be Matt?” he said as he shook his hand.
“Yes indeed. Nice to meet you.”
“Nice to meet you too. It’s a lovely old house, isn’t it? I guess you probably noticed, there are three

cottages, but numbers Two and Three will not be vacant for some time as they're in need of refurbishment, but number One is up for sale. It was refurbished several decades ago, shortly after the pub was rebuilt," Craig explained.
"Actually," put in Matt, "I know the cottage well. I used to know the family who lived here, but that's a long time ago though."
"Oh?" said Craig, He paused for a moment and then, unfazed, went on with his sales patter. He sounded as if he'd memorised the property specifications. "Previously, it's been rented out as a holiday-let due to its perfect location. It has everything on its doorstep and I'm sure your guests would love to stay down here. The row of cottages stands on the original plot of land once owned by Deryk Carver, the founder of The Black Lion. He was a well known brewer in East Sussex distributing his beer to many pubs in the area. His brown beer was a godsend to the locals. He was so well known that even today people mention his name, keeping his spirit alive so to speak."
Craig opened the black wooden front door, leading straight into the lounge. There was an open kitchen and stairs on their right, leading up to the other rooms. "Feel free to have a look around. I'll wait here until you've finished. Any questions, just

shout!”
It was a long time since Matt and his friend had climbed the narrow stairs to play in the cosy rooms upstairs. Strangely enough, neither his childhood friend nor his family had mentioned anything about the history of the pub and its founder, Deryk Carver. These cottages dated back to the sixteenth century. Surely they must have known?
From an adult perspective, Matt thought the unfurnished cottage had a lot of potential, and it had all the amenities it needed for a holiday let including the white goods. All it needed was new furniture and a good lick of paint. It would probably take him a month to do it up before advertising it.
“I like it,” he said to Craig, coming back down the narrow stairs. “I would like to make an offer.”
“Thank you. I’ll let my client know and get back to you over the next couple of days.” They shook hands and left.

The following week Matt received a phone call from Craig telling him that the seller had accepted his offer under the condition that their name not be disclosed. When Matt received the documents from his solicitor, with a completion date in a month’s time, by the end of July, he was overcome with excitement at the idea of becoming the new owner of a four hundred year old cottage. The same evening he opened a bottle of champagne and celebrated this special occasion with his friends into the early hours. Should he resign from his current role, or should he try and run it in his spare time? Matt chose the latter, and by going part-time, he managed to run the holiday-let. And in no time, the bookings were rolling in.

Welcome to Black Lion Cottage.

In the wooden chest on the coffee table you'll find an envelope with a set of keys. The long silver key gives you access to the main bedroom and the smaller black keys are for the smaller bedrooms. The key with the black label can be used to open and lock the patio.
The kitchen units are stocked with essentials like tea, coffee, sugar, breakfast bars. In the fridge you'll find milk and butter. There's a kettle, coffee machine, toaster, cooking facilities and a microwave. The cutlery can be found in the drawers and pans in the unit below. On the kitchen table you'll find some brochures about Brighton, bus service, taxis, pubs and restaurants. Smoking in the cottage is prohibited but feel free to smoke in the patio area. If you're interested in the history of Brighton you can visit the museum, Jubilee Library or if you dare, The Black Lion pub next door where the ghost of founder Deryk Carver is reputed to move barrels of beer around in the cellars and has been sighted at an upstairs window in the mid 90s...

I live locally and am on hand should you need me.

Enjoy your stay!

Matt

Booking One

In medieval England, the wives of sea fishermen working in perilous waters believed that keeping a black cat would protect their husbands while they were away. Others, however, believed that cats were in fact witches disguised in animal form.

Gerald was a self-employed driving instructor. One night, he went on a blind date and met Faye, an occupational therapist. They went to the Theatre Royal in Brighton and watched the musical *Cats* together. During the interval, they chatted about the songs and the plot, discussing the part where the leader of a tribe chooses a cat to ascend to the Heaviside layer to be reborn. Gerald confessed that he was not a big cat lover – "I was once attacked by a cat," he laughed – but despite this, the pair got on well. So well, in fact, that they married not too long after.

Many years later, as they were arranging to visit their daughter Sylvia and their grandson Dom in Brighton, Gerald was busy browsing the internet for suitable accommodation. To his surprise, all the hotels were fully booked, except for a Holiday Let in the city centre. He emailed Matt and was relieved to find the cottage was still available for rent.

It was mid-morning when Gerald and Faye drove down the A23 towards the coast. The sky was clouded with hardly a glimpse of a dim sun as they drew up in Brighton.
At the end of a dark and quiet narrow lane, they reached their destination. A creaking sign above the door advertised *Black Lion Cottage.* Entering the cottage, they walked into the charming atmosphere of the past. It had classic oak-beamed ceilings, a medium window letting in natural light and a neat pile of chopped wood stacked against the back of the house. They dropped off their suitcases and went straight out to The Cricketers next door for some pub grub. They sat in the enclosed cobblestoned courtyard, admiring the wood-framed windows with their tied-back red velvet curtains with golden silk tassels. It was as if they had stepped back into Victorian times.
"It's good to be back, isn't it?" said Gerald, as he put down his glass of fizz.
"It is indeed," said Faye happily, "and such a wonderful start to our mini-break, especially in *this* pub. It's one of the oldest in Brighton, isn't it?"
Gerald nodded. A thought struck him and he reached into his pocket for a little brochure. "Oh, I

forgot to tell you, I found this on the coffee table. I had a quick glance at it - it's about Preston Park. Apparently, there's a secret garden next to Preston Manor – you remember, that historic house we used to visit? Do you think Dom might be interested in exploring it?"
"I'm sure he would love it," said Faye. "He's a little adventurer."
Gerald and Faye paid the bill, walked to the Lanes car park and drove up to Preston Park to meet Sylvia and Dom.
"Mum and dad, how lovely to see you!"
"How lovely to see *you* too," said Faye, giving her daughter a kiss and a big hug.
"How's my brave grandson?" Gerald pinched Dom's cheeks. The little boy jumped up and down, very excited to see him.
After a cup of tea and cake, Gerald decided to take Dom for a walk in the park, leaving Faye to stay behind with her daughter to catch up on all the latest gossip.

Gerald's mind went back to an evening nearly two decades before in this very same road. It was after a difficult driving lesson: he had dropped off a pupil at her flat after braving an unexpected snowstorm in the dark. As a result, the lesson had taken longer

than he had anticipated and all Gerald had wanted was to go home and relax. Clearly agitated, he had started the car, driving off at high speed; but just then, a creature had run in front of the car. In a flash, he could see its eyes lit by the headlights, briefly glancing at him before it was hit by the vehicle. He had braked fiercely, the car screeching to a halt.
It was quiet: most people had stayed indoors due to the icy weather. Gerald jumped out of the car and followed the tyre marks in the snow. He looked around. Strangely enough, there was no casualty to be found, neither were there any traces of blood. Could it have been a cat? Cats are known to have nine lives. They say cats can withstand falls and other serious accidents without being fatally wounded. Gerald, guessing it must have had a lucky escape, had climbed back into his car and driven away. He felt relieved – but someone was left devastated the following day.

Dawn's alarm went off at 7:00 am. She put on her dressing gown and walked down the stairs into the kitchen to feed her cat. She took a bowl, put fresh food into it and put it down on the floor. "Felicia? Where are you? Mummy got foodies for you."
Dawn made herself a cup of coffee and sat down.

After she finished her cup there was still no cat to be seen. She looked at the cat flap and it was then she started to worry. Her poor Felicia hadn't come home, the first time in nine years. She opened the backdoor to search the snowy garden, shivering in the cold. "Felicia darling, where are you? Come to mummy!"
Dawn peeped over the fencing into her neighbours' gardens, but there was no sign of her cat. In tears, she phoned her friend Jules and told her Felicia had gone missing.
"Poor you! Let's hope she turns up soon. When was the last time you saw her?" asked Jules.
"Yesterday afternoon. She brought back a dead bird. She can't help it – you know that cats possess a natural instinct to hunt and she just wants to share her catch with her loved one. I did tell her off and gave her a meal before she went back outside through the cat flap. She's a typical outdoor cat, you know, but it's completely out of character that she hasn't returned."
"Well, I suggest you report her missing to the vet and the microchip database. I'm keeping my fingers crossed for you!"
"I'll do that. Thank you. Speak soon." Dawn put down the phone and reported Felicia as missing before she left for work.

She started the engine of her car and drove off, turning into Preston Road. As she passed the bus stop, she spotted something black lying on the pavement. Immediately she brought the car to a halt and hastily got out, leaving the engine running. Her shaking hands held to her mouth, she hurried towards the thing on the floor, dreading to see Felicia. Next to the bin she saw the frozen body of her dearly beloved cat.

"Oh my God!" These were the only words Dawn could speak before her eyes welled up. She knelt down beside the lifeless little black animal, tears rolling down her cheeks. She lifted her up, and decided to take Felicia's body to the secret garden next to Preston Manor.

Dawn was familiar with the rumours about the site, having lived locally for a long time. Some said the church grounds were cursed. Some said it had its own 'Death Tree' standing in the middle of the graveyard and that if a person waited there until the darkest hours, they would hear agonising groans emanating from the tree. The secret garden, situated at the other side of the lawn overlooked by the church, had a forgotten corner devoted to the graves of animals, pets who had once lived in the Manor House in days long gone by. Dawn sobbed loudly as she buried the remains of Felicia secretively in the snowy little pet cemetery that day. Deep in her heart she hoped and believed that one day her pet would return, in the body of another cat; and all the while, she vowed to get revenge on Felicia's murderer.

Gerald, who had put aside the memory of the strange incident on that long-ago snowy night, crossed Preston Road, holding little Dom's hand, to enter the large urban park.
"Several years ago," he told his grandson, "on a stormy day, your grandma and I visited Preston Manor. Has your mum taken you to have a look already?"
"No, Grandad," said Dom.
"Well, the brochure I found in our holiday cottage says that it has a long history of ghostly phenomena and paranormal experiences. That means spooky things happen there!" Seeing that Dom was listening with interest, Gerald continued the story.
"The family who lived there were called the Stanfords and they had a lot of trouble with two ghosts. Just imagine, a lady in white, used to be seen wandering through the burial grounds behind the old church, frightening the children! And a second one, a lady in grey, used to glide down the main stairs and disappeared into nowhere! Several guests

told stories of how they had seen disembodied hands on the bedposts, and one said he'd heard weird and uncanny noises coming from the big dress cupboard."

"That sounds scary, Grandad. Are the ghosts still there?"

Gerald laughed to reassure his grandson. "I don't believe it one bit! And anyway, it happened a long time ago, Dom, and people believe the souls of the dead have moved on and have found peace. Why don't we follow the gravel pathway from the old church towards the gardens next to the old manor to see it for ourselves?"

Gerald took Dom's hand and after a short stroll, crossing the green lawns, they arrived in front of a black iron gate set in a brick arch. Somehow, there was a charm about this old fashioned garden with herbaceous borders and shrubs growing between the gravel paths. In the middle of it, he spotted a black cat sitting, licking its paw. The cat looked up. It stared at Gerald in a sinister manner, clearly discouraging their approach.

Gerald, distracted by the muffled sound of fast moving traffic on Preston Road, turned his head and watched the cars go by in the distance. The contrast between the distant sound of the traffic and the silence in the garden gave a strange sense of being

in two different worlds. Gerald looked back at the gate and to his surprise, it had been opened, but the cat had disappeared. Did it just suddenly run off? Gerald feeling a little bit unnerved, took his grandson by his hand, and slowly walked down the steps into the tranquil walled garden. The flints and mortar on the walls had weathered and plant life had grown in the crevices, giving them an ancient appearance. In the middle of the mesmerising green stood a gold sundial, glistening in the sunlight, framed by an old-looking arch which curved gracefully over one of the paths. The garden was filled with the beautiful scent of flowers and roses, and there were sweet and lemony scented water lilies floating in a sunken pond.
Gerald and Dom walked past a wall where red climbing roses scrambled up the old flints, drawing them to a much greater height than they would have grown elsewhere. They inhaled the sweet, intense, and floral fragrance of the large blooms. Hidden between the overgrown plants and beautiful flowers, Gerald spotted a group of tiny mysterious stones, standing close up against the stone wall. They had discovered a small pet cemetery with tiny gravestones, nestled among the plants, a touching window into the past. Immediately, Dom was fascinated by the little memorials, and knelt down in

front of a small bush, studying the names of the dogs and when they had died. A sudden rustling sound came from the shrub in front of him. He peeked into it, and just as he moved the branches aside, a pair of vicious yellow eyes became visible, staring at him. Within seconds a black creature leapt from the bush, straight over Dom's shoulder, landing on the path behind him. The cat glanced with a cold look at Gerald, hissing at him with its ears back and flat against its head. Then it disappeared behind the wall.

"That cat really made me jump! You should have seen the look in its eyes. Dom, are you okay?"

"Yes, I'm fine Grandad." Dom nodded his head and knelt down again, fascinated by the pet cemetery, slowly counting all of its little tombstones. At least sixteen dogs and three cats were laid to rest in the walled flower garden, all lined up against the wall and the little tombstones commemorating the pets of the Manor's previous owners, the Stanford family. On one stone Dom read: *To the memory of my dear and faithful dogs Little Rags and Fritz..* The animals seemed to come to life before Dom's eyes, as he imagined their behaviours, characters.

"Grandad, I can see Little Rags. He was a Scottish terrier. He's so funny. His hair is sweeping the ground and he's making me laugh." Dom giggled.

"He looks like a walking mop head! And Fritz is a dachshund, barking at anyone and anything, so loud, the male household staff are wearing ear-plugs!"

Gerald, seeing how interested Dom was in the graves and listening to his imaginative descriptions of the pets, read aloud from the brochure he'd kept in his pocket. "Listen to this, Dom! This one here is Peter, a Yorkshire terrier, laid beside Fritz, remembered by the words: *In Memory of Dear Peter, Who was Cross and Sulky, but Loved us.*

Dom giggled to himself as he imagined the little dog had a bad habit of biting anyone wearing a white apron. He though how if the Lady of the manor had ever disguised herself as a maid, that naughty dog would be so cross and sulky that he'd bite her as well. Since the family's passing, it seemed some people had added little tombstones commemorating their own pets deaths. Perhaps the saddest memorial of them all was dedicated to a cat, Felicia, which was found dead on 7th March 2002.

For nine years, Felicia was my friend and playmate. A cat has nine lives. For three she played, for three she strayed, and for the last three she stayed. I hope she's playing elsewhere now.

Feeling a little tired, Gerard sat himself down on a green wooden bench nearby.
"That's a good boy, Dom, you just have a look at those little gravestones while your old grandfather has a sit down." He breathed deeply, drawing in the sweet scent of flowers and listening to the birdsong.
"Grandad, look!" Dom was suddenly next to him, tugging at his sleeve. He was pointing at a fresh hole dug into the grave of the cat. "Who would have dug up an old grave like that? Maybe someone's been burying secret treasure there?"
Gerard, smiling at his imaginative grandson, decided to humour him. "Let's find out," he said, kneeling down next to the small hole and gingerly sticking his hand into the soil.
He felt something, and picked it up. After he brushed of the mud, he could see it was a name tag, engraved with the cat's name: *Felicia.*
At the same moment Gerald heard a piercing noise and looked behind him. The black iron gate had been shut. The handle was still vibrating in the lock. Dom's body was shaking and Gerald put his arms around his grandson, holding him very tight. The silence was broken by a yowl coming from a tree. A pair of bright yellow eyes was staring at Gerald. Ever since they had set foot in the secret gardens,

Gerald has been pestered by this creature. What was going on?
"Grandad, what's that over there?" Dom looked scared, pointing his finger at the laburnum tunnel-arch. Gerald saw a woman, wearing a long black cloak, slowly walking towards them, beneath a cascade of golden blossoms. The cat, still staring at Gerald, jumped from the branch in front of the little tombstone. Gerald wondered why the same cat had followed him around from the moment he arrived at the gate, giving him evil looks. What did it want from him? The cat, unpredictably, sprinted towards the woman, curled itself around her leg. A hand appeared from underneath her cloak, stroking the purring feline. "My little friend," she murmured, "you hardly need to speak. Your eyes tell me everything."
The cat was now gazing at Gerald, as it sat in the grass, staring fixedly at him, as if it was stalking prey. He could read its mind.
"Come on, Dom, I have a feeling we should get back to see your mum and Grandma." He took Dom by the hand and walked back towards the black iron gate. Out of the corner of his eye, he seemed to see the woman gliding uncannily through the garden with the cat at her heels. Gerald was shocked to find them abruptly standing right in front of them. The

woman stared at him furiously but spoke in a strange, soft voice.

"Before you go, there's something you need to hear from me. This is my cat, Felicia. You've met her before. On a cold winter's evening many years ago, she did not have a lucky escape after somebody hit her with his car. Do you happen to know anything about it?"

"What do you mean?" Gerald snapped at her, taken by surprise. He had an odd feeling of being rooted to the spot, unable to move a muscle. Unwillingly, he was forced to listen silently as the woman's words sunk into his mind.

"It's my intuition, I can feel and see the revealed truth without conscious reasoning, just like cats. They are very intuitive and sensitive animals. One evening, around twenty years ago, you dropped off your last pupil, you drove back home through Preston Road, and hit Felicia just as she was crossing the road. The poor thing was flung across the road, in a state of total agony, ending up next to the bus shelter. She was still alive when you drove off, but instead you left her to freeze to death during that cold winter night.

It was me who found her body the next morning, and I buried her remains in this cursed secret garden."

"That's complete nonsense!" Gerald laughed. "This simply can't be true. If this happened twenty years ago the cat wouldn't be alive today, would she?"
"That evening you believed that cats can withstand falls and other serious accidents without being fatally wounded. A cat has nine lives, remember? It's ironic that you're here today with somebody who is so dear to your heart, your grandson. You know, Felicia was so dear to my heart too.
All that is left of her now is her ghost, trapped in this damned park. I thought she had completed her nine lives but, apparently, she 'whispered' to me she still has one life left." The woman stared at Gerald. Her look was cold and terrifying. Like an arrow from a bow, the cat jumped from behind the woman, claws open wide, pouncing on Gerald's face. Just before Felicia tried to sink her sharp nails deep into his eyes, Gerald woke up.
He was sitting on the green wooden bench in the walled garden next to his grandson, looking a little bit bewildered, clearly remembering every detail of his horrible dream.
"Grandad, you've woken up! I was a little bit worried, you were mumbling in your sleep, but I couldn't understand what you were trying to say."
"Don't worry Dom," he said relieved, "your grandfather was just having a dream."

"Look, I got something for you!" Dom was holding up a collar.
"Give it to Grandad so I can have a look at it."
Gerald was astonished when he read the name on the tag. *Felicia.* "Please, tell me, where exactly did you find this, Dom?"
"I didn't find it, Grandpa. A woman gave it to me." Dom's face looked mystified. "She just left, but she told me to give it to you as soon as you woke up."
Gerald panicked. Did he dream the whole thing, or was it real? Anxiously, he scanned the garden. "Tell me quickly, where did she go?"
"She walked through the gate."
Gerald took Dom by his hand and swiftly walked towards the gate. He pushed his shoulder against it, but it wouldn't open. It was locked. He scanned the walls. There must be another way out, he thought. Behind the evergreen bushes, was a wall with a semi circular brick arch with a green open door. Gerald sprinted to the arch, keeping Dom close behind him, rushing through it. They ran across the park as fast as they could, reaching the kerb next to the main road. Focussed on getting back to Sylvia's flat, they crossed Preston Road. Out of the blue, a car approached at a very high speed. The last thing Gerald heard was an ear-piercing revving sound before it deliberately careered towards them,

plunging into Dom.

The driver, who must have noticed the collision, looked into the side mirror, and could see a man sitting down in the middle of the road holding the body of the child. She stopped the car next to the pavement, the engine still running, and a mirthless smile appeared on her face. Dawn glanced over her shoulder and watched her cat lying on the backseat, stretching out its paws, asking for some affection and she gladly obliged. Stroking him, she looked into his blue eyes, they looked almost human. It was as if there was a person stuck in its body. Cats don't seem to give up their ghost easily. "Hello sweetie, you like that, don't you?" The cat made calming, purring sounds, closed its eyes, and opened them slowly with the appearance of feline contentment. Before she pressed the accelerator, Dawn said. "Well, I think we're going to pay a visit to the pet shop to get you a collar and a new name tag, I'll ask them to engrave the name Dom on it."

Deryk

It was misty when I left Liège, a city situated at the foot of Ardennes Forest, on the river Meuse. Gothic cathedrals, imposing palaces, and timber townhouses were built on the high rolling hills and ridges, at the backdrop of the endless dense woods. From the vessel I looked back, remembering how I used to walk through the shady narrow streets in the old town of Dilson by Stockome, the place I was born. I used to play at skipping rope and games of marbles with the boys and girls. My favourite game was Hide and Seek - my friends never managed to find me. I had a secret hiding-place in the Benedictine Abbey, where my father worked. It was here that I eventually learned the craft of brewing. My father was an established and well-known brewer in Flanders where many local pubs served his ales and beers. Occasionally we had to leave the city and travel by horse and cart through the city gates to deliver barrels of beer to nearby villages in rural areas. My father told me how lucky I was to have the opportunity to become a brewer. Only a few people practised this profession. At the time the situation between the Catholic and Protestant church was getting very tense. A period of Catholic resurgence was initiated in response to the Protestant Reformation to protect the power, influence, and wealth of the Catholic Church. They were on the brink of war.

My family was worried about my future as a Protestant, and made the difficult decision to send me abroad, hoping I would be safe. My father, a wealthy man, arranged for me to sail to England, taking with me an iron money box filled with a sufficient supply of gold sovereigns and silver shillings to start a brewery. Several days before my departure, my father had purchased the coins from a money exchanger at the market square next to the river. Many of them had found their way to the cities of Bruges, Antwerp, and Liège. Considering the enormous variety of clothes, spices and coal the traders brought with them into the countries, you can imagine there were a lot of coins in circulation. The iron money box and its contents were on board the vessel hidden in a safe place. Travelling via the river was a safer option as there was a high risk of getting robbed if we travelled over land.

On the day of my departure the mist was moving up the slopes of the hill as the vessel sailed on the morning tide, following the flow of the river Meuse. Through the low clouds I gazed at the cathedrals, looking like phantoms standing on the hills. The towers on the high city walls and the bastions dwindled into the distance as the winding leg of our journey went on, until they disappeared from view.

I felt a lump growing in my throat, my eyes welled up: an adult man, trying hard not to cry. I realised I had just left everything behind, my family, my friends, my town, and my childhood. It was a closed chapter with many good and some bad memories. I felt a little melancholy, but my feelings gradually turned into excitement when I thought about crossing the sea together with all the men on this vessel. A new life lay ahead of me. I passed the beautiful hills of Maastricht followed by views of small villages lining the river banks, some rising starkly from the river's edge. The vessel ended in the Port of Antwerp, gaining its fame at this time, it was the commercial heart of Europe, called the Diamond Capital due to its trade in these valuable crystals. The pear shaped ship, called a fluyt, was similar to that of the early galleons. It had a large cargo bay near the waterline and a relatively narrow deck above. It was square rigged with three masts which were much higher than those of galleons to allow for greater speed.

Just before the vessel reached the sea, there was a chilly breeze, and the flags on the top of the pole started to flap.

'Stay, Deryk', someone whispered to me.

Instantly I recognised her voice, it was my late grand-mother.

'Stay with your family. Get off the ship before it's too late!'

The wind was picking up. An unexpected strong gust tore

a flag fr[illegible] fully fluttered down, landing b[illegible]r going up and down my spine. In fr[illegible]ag of Flanders, carrying the image of the [illegible]ike the painting which used to hang in my gr[illegible]r's living room. I was holding on to the flag w[illegible]sel entered the waters to sail to the Dover Narro[illegible]ew she was with me, trying to protect me.

'Should you want to cross, smell the sea, and feel the sky, who am I to stop you? If this is what you want, then let your spirit fly'.

I could hear my grand-mother's wise words and sweet voice echoing in my mind, but I had made my choice, there was no turning back. I couldn't turn back.

The sky was clear and the sea was dead calm, and then, I saw the beautiful white cliffs of Dover, rising like a phoenix from the water.

They had a striking appearance: soaring cliffs towering over three hundred feet in height, composed of white chalk, a sight I'd never seen before, stretching for eight miles at the point where Britain is closest to continental Europe. Without realising it, I had sealed my own fate, not knowing I would die in this beautiful country because of a change in religion, and my own stubbornness. I was a Protestant and I held on to my belief. It was my own choice, but thinking about it now, I wonder why? Heretics were burned if they refused to recant. And so it happened *to me. But, if I had been allowed to enter heaven, as they describe it, I wouldn't be sitting here, telling you my story. In the end, maybe each person's destiny is a thread spun, measured, and cut by the three Fates, the mythical sisters Moira. The Greeks called them Clotho, Lachesis and Atropos. They said that Clotho spins the thread of life, Lachesis measures it, and Atropos cuts it, determining the individual's moment of death: eventually choosing my death.*

Booking Two

Guy was an HR manager, and his wife Isabel was a mother and part-time head of Social Care and Health. They resided in Cambridge with their three children Angela (just turning fourteen), Tom (eleven) and Rupert (nine). Whilst all their children were sensitive to 'atmospheres' and paranormal activity, it was especially Tom who seemed to be more perceptive. One day he said he had seen a very old man in their house, describing him in precise detail. He even explained that he carried a white cotton handkerchief in his pocket embroidered with the initial E. Only Isabel knew her late father carried an identical one in memory of his wife Elizabeth. Both her parents had died and there were no photographs or images of them as they were lost in a fire before Tom was even born. After that, sometimes Isabel wondered if Tom was fully grounded in everyday reality. She often noticed how deeply he became absorbed in psychic events and would sometimes casually talk about people and things that she could not see, as if they were part of normal everyday experience. She and Guy chose never to question these occasionally-strange narratives, but nevertheless, they kept an eye on him. Tom definitely had a very special gift. And secretly, she worried that such a gift might be fraught with its own dangers as he was such a trusting child.

Guy and Isabel, desperately in need of a break from their stressful lives, decided to book a holiday cottage for a long-weekend escape with their children. After a three hour journey, they arrived at the cottage, one of the oldest properties in Brighton. The cottage was relatively small compared to their large three storey family home, but it was full of tiny decor details, and they immediately fell in love with it. Guy took their suitcases and bags, climbed the very narrow steps leading up to the bedrooms, and dropped them on the bed. Above the bed hung a dramatic painting of an old wooden structure with a peaked roof set along the coast. Guy paused for a moment to look more closely at the picture, speculating that building's dim attic was probably creaky and full of cobwebs and spiders. Who would want to live in such a place, overlooking the sea? He was still distracted by his thoughts when he heard someone coming up the stairs.
It was Isabel. "I've just told Angela that an extra pair of hands will make putting everything away so much easier," she said as she began opening one of the

suitcases. "So, I've left her in charge of making coffee. She's so grown up now, she should be able to manage it." She glanced across at her husband with a wry smile.
"Fingers crossed!" laughed Guy.
It didn't take long to empty out their suitcases. When Isabel closed the wardrobe she could smell the aroma of fresh coffee coming from downstairs. Back down in the open plan kitchen they nestled themselves on the sofa next to their sons who were playing games on their tablets, whilst Angela served them the drinks and biscuits.
"Brilliant job with the coffee, Angie!" said Guy.
"It's great to be near the sea, isn't it?" Isabel looked at the happy faces of her children. "And .. we have a surprise for you. After we've finished our coffees we'll be heading over to Hove for a meal at the Hangleton Manor to celebrate Angela's birthday!"
Angela, Tom, and Rupert cheered with excitement.
"We're taking you there for a special reason. I've done some research and the story goes the manor is haunted. I have read that many guests have felt cold spots in the restaurant, or heard creaking noises coming from the floor above whilst having their dinner. I bet you can't wait to see it."

After a twenty minute ride they arrived at the Manor.

The children jumped out of the car, and ran towards the entrance. Angela and Rupert were ahead of Tom. Just before reaching the entrance, he tripped over a stone, lost his balance, and fell over.
"Ouch!" he cried. He had hurt his knees. Angela and Rupert stopped and immediately ran back to check up on their brother.
"Tom, are you ok?" asked Angela.
"Do you need a hand, bruv?" Rupert said, concerned.
"Thank you. I'm okay." Tom grimaced with pain. "It looks like my knees are grazed, that's all." When he put out his hands to push himself up, he felt a small green bag beside him. Curious to find out what was inside of it, he picked up the bag, opening it. To his surprise it was filled with marbles: white, yellow and brown marbles.
"Look!" Tom showed them the contents of the bag. Angela peeked into it. "Oh my gosh! It's full of marbles. They look like ancient marbles. It looks like they're really old."
"I think you're right, sis. I just knew they were special. I'm so glad I found them."
They stood under the hanging black lantern at the entrance to the hotel and looked at the building. The two-storey porch was flint-built with a gabled roof. Tom's eyes were studying the old knapped

flint stone wall, fascinated by the old structure. On the two-storey wing of the house he counted eight bays with sash windows, overlooking the Manor's driveway. Tucked just under the roof, Tom spotted a small latticed attic window, the ones you see in old churches or abbeys. It was slightly opened, and the curtains swayed gently dancing with the breeze. But then someone pulled back the curtains. Instinctively Tom stepped back to get a better view. He saw a boy appearing in the window, wearing a white shirt. Tom's eyes were locked on him.
'*Come and play with us in the attic,*' the boy whispered.
Tom looked at the boy in a casual way, it was not the first time he had encountered a ghost, but he wondered whether it was a good thing to go upstairs? He wasn't familiar with the lay-out of the restaurant, and the boy appeared to be in the private living quarters two floors above it. How was he supposed to get there?
Tom heard a loud voice. It was his father. "Tom, look at your knees and your clothes. We're about to have dinner! Be careful next time, don't run before you can walk."
"I'll be more careful next time, dad," said Tom, looking back at the attic window. The window was closed. The boy had disappeared, but the curtains were still swaying. It was then he realised the boy

must have been real, inviting him to play in the attic.

The family dined in style in the grand hall, seated beneath a wall carving of the Ten Commandments. Everything - from the dark oak ceiling beams and cathedral candle holders to the wall mounted stags heads - created a medieval atmosphere. After they had finished their three course dinner the manager came over to their table. He was a large comfortable-looking man with glasses and wispy grey hair. He had an old-fashioned air and spoke in a slow, deliberate style, as though he enjoyed choosing his words judiciously. Now he looked at his guests kindly. "Happy birthday to you, Angela. I hope you enjoyed your meal?"
"Yes, it was delicious, thank you."
"I'm pleased to hear that, and I hope you liked the venue as well?"
"I did. It's the perfect setting for a birthday party. When we drove down I googled your venue and read that people have seen ghosts at the Manor. I hope you don't mind me asking, but do you happen to know anything about this?"
"Well, everyday I get many requests from mediums, psychics, and spiritual people from all over Britain. They want to connect with the ghosts of previous occupants who died here centuries ago. There are

quite a few hidden rooms in the Manor which have been closed for many years as they were no longer safe to enter. They say they're haunted."
"I'm sorry to interrupt," Tom said, "but is the small attic room above the entrance closed too?"
"Indeed it is, like most of the rooms on the first and second floor. It was originally the home of the High Sheriff of Sussex, who built it in the mid-sixteenth century, and travelled between this town and London. Did you know that the original village of Hangleton was situated on an ancient trackway coming from London? The road used to go through the old village of Portslade. Previous owners of the Manor opened up the upstairs rooms to travellers and used it as a hotel, but it didn't last very long. Apparently many guests said the upstairs rooms were haunted and they claimed that ghosts were keeping them awake at night."
"That's interesting," Angela frowned. "So people suspected there was ghost activity in the Manor?"
"I wouldn't rule out any ghost activity," the manager said." Allegedly, one of the guests claimed they had seen a rocking horse creaking away on the landing during the night. Other guests who stayed here said they'd seen ghosts in the bedrooms, the hallway, and in the garden, and soon the word spread. People became afraid and stayed away. Eventually the

rooms in the hotel remained empty and unfortunately they had to close them down."
Angela lowered her eyes. "That's such a sad thing to do. Most ghosts don't cause any harm. I can feel their presence, right here, and I can tell you about their past lives. Can you feel it too?"
"I'm afraid I don't. You must be a psychic child?" The manager looked at Angela, intrigued. "I've read a book on understanding children's psychic gifts and their startling stories of contact with deceased family members from beyond the grave. I thought it was fascinating." Angela, rather enjoying the attention, glanced round at her family and prepared to expand on the subject. Ever since last year, she had been keeping a secret journal where she would write thoughtfully about her own experiences and had struggled to find words to describe the family gift. Now, she thought, was an opportunity to use the phrases she was proud to have found.
"I'm sensitive to atmospheres and paranormal activity, just like my brothers. At home I've made contact with deceased family members and neighbours. The first time was scary, as I didn't know what to do. You suddenly find yourself in a tranquil space between the past and present. It almost felt unreal, but I taught myself how to connect with the spirits from the past, and instead of being scary, it

feels more like being in harmony. It's like that beautiful feeling you get when you hear two violins playing, blending their frequencies together, creating an energy which pleases your ears, and fills your mind with strong feelings of love."

"The words you have used to describe this phenomenon are beautifully chosen. You're a very bright girl!" said the manager. "I understand what you're saying, and I believe people can be in good harmony with ghosts, but unfortunately, I've also been told that some are evil, and can hide behind any corner. On that note, I've heard rumours about ghost sightings around the old church up the hill. Please take my advice, don't ever go there! Even the locals tend to stay away from it. Well, I hope you enjoyed your evening, young lady. Please, excuse me, but I have to see to my other diners. Perhaps, one day, you could return with your family, and tell me all about the previous occupants who died centuries ago? I would be very interested."

Angela looked at the approving faces of her parents, smiling at her. "Thank you. I would love to!"

"Excuse me, dad." Tom attracted his father's attention. "Please may I leave the table? I need to use the toilet."

"Of course you can," Guy smiled, "but don't get any ideas running off to that church up the hill."

Tom fully intended to go straight to the toilet and then return to the dining table. He entered the dimly-lit hallway, where the mirror, reflecting the light of the mounted lanterns onto the walls, created sufficient light to navigate the passage. On his left, there was a door slightly ajar. The sign on it read: *Do not enter*. There was nobody around and he peeked through the crack. What he saw was intriguing beyond belief. Rising from the ground was a grand dark brown wooden staircase, inviting him to enter the mysterious unknown parts of the Manor. Inquisitively and quite forgetting why he had left his family, Tom walked up the wide steps. The first thing he saw was a dramatic-looking old bronze chandelier with candles hanging from the high ceiling above him. Behind the huge paned window, he saw a golden-yellow moon crescent, shining its pale light in the evening sky. There were oil paintings hanging on the wall in gilded picture frames. He could just make out images of shipwrecks, portraits of men and women, and a painting of a black lion. Impressed with what he had seen, Tom followed the steps up the winding staircase. On the top of the solid newels stood two candles, flickering like little islands in a sea of darkness, giving the space a warm glow. In front of him were several doors with gold key chains hanging from the door handles. Tom recalled the conversation between his sister Angela and the manager. These must be the hotel rooms he talked about where the guests had seen ghosts, closed for many years in the belief the Manor was haunted. He looked to his right and discovered a second staircase. Tom felt scared, but at the same time he remembered the boy he'd seen, inviting him to come up and play, and he began hoping it would lead to the attic. He climbed the steep wooden staircase, each step making a squeaking noise, leading to a hatch which opened to another room. Looking ahead, he immediately identified the small attic window in the moonlight, he saw five small beds, a rocking horse, whistles, and several dolls. Suddenly Tom heard the sound of bouncing marbles. It reminded him of the small bag he had found outside, and he put his hand in his pocket. He couldn't feel the green bag. Where had it gone? He searched his other pocket too, but it had disappeared. He must have lost it. The room felt eerie. He was cold and sweaty, and felt cobwebs on his face.

In desperate need of fresh air, Tom drew the curtains apart, and opened the windows. The fresh air gradually filled the room and he started to feel better. After he had calmed down and was just beginning to wonder if he had imagined the sound of bouncing marbles, he heard footsteps. They were quickly moving backwards and forwards, and there was the sound of talking and giggling. Tom stood still and listened. The sounds were real, he hadn't imagined it. Marbles were being dropped on the floor, bouncing and rolling. At the same moment, Tom looked at the sky and held his breath. A silhouette was floating in the air, steady at first, but in the next second everything changed. Tom felt helpless as the silhouette approached the attic, moving through the open windows into the room. Tom stood with his back against the wall, shivering, feeling the blood drain from his face. In the middle of the room, stood a boy, with dark cropped hair. He was probably Tom's own age. Instantly, Tom recognised him: it was the same boy he had been searching for, the one who had whispered to him from this very window.

'Hello, I'm Ed. What's your name?'

"Hi, my name is Tom. I remember you."

'Yes, I remember you too, you were looking at me. I asked you to come and play. Do you have any brothers or sisters?'

"I have a sister and a brother. What about you?"

'I have four sisters. We were playing marbles and I won all of them. I really like the one with the ghost

in it.'
"Well done for winning the game, I bet your sisters must have been gutted!" Tom was not in the least surprised to find himself chatting comfortably to his new friend. It was all so dreamlike and he had known as soon as he saw the boy's face at the window that they could be good mates. "So tell me, what is it you like about the one with the ghost in it?"
'My father Richard once said, each marble contains a great mystery. He said if you look closely, you will see a white shadow frozen in the gallery of time in each one. Do you play marbles? If so, can I see them?'
"I love playing marbles too, but I'm afraid I don't have them on me. Do your sisters happen to be here too?"
'No, they've left. They've gone to the old church, up the hill. Would you like to meet them? The church is only across the field?'
"I was told by my father and the manager of the restaurant not to go there. The manager of the restaurant talked about evil spirits hiding behind any corner - or at least, I think that's what he said. But I'm curious and keen to visit the church because I want to meet your sisters. I'm sure my brother and sister would want to come too. I'll ask them. Give me a couple of minutes and I'll meet you

outside!"
Tom rushed back to the restaurant. He could hardly wait to tell Angela and Rupert about his new friend, although he felt a slight misgiving that he had probably been gone far longer than he should. To his surprise, he found his sister and brother still sitting at the table, looking bored and eating ice cream, whilst his parents were standing over at the service counter with the manager, poring over an old book.
"Oh, finally, the wanderer returns!" said Angela sarcastically. "We were just about to send out a search party for you."
"Lucky for you that mum and dad got distracted by the manager," said Rupert."They got all excited just because he asked them to look at some old book or something. Really boring. But we got seconds of ice cream, any flavour we want. I had *all* the flavours. I think yours has melted."
Regretfully ignoring the ice cream, Tom told them about his meeting with Ed and the exciting chance to have a look at the church. "Come on, let's do it. Mum and Dad won't even notice we've gone. And it's not far."
"Hang on, hang on!" said Angela. "They expressly forbade us to go to the church and if you two wander off, I'll be the one to get the blame." She

glanced shrewdly at her parents again. The manager seemed to have brought out a second large and battered tome for inspection. "But they're going to be ages yet, I can just tell. And," she added brightly, "it *is* my birthday and I am now fourteen, which everyone knows is a very responsible age to be, because it's when you have to choose your exam subjects. So I'll look after you two. I'll tell them we're just going to get some fresh air and that I'm totally in charge of everything."

After Angela had used her powers of persuasion on Guy and Isabel, the children made their way outside where they found Tom's new friend.

Ed had the appearance of a normal boy of about Tom's age, but Angela noticed that his simple clothing was indefinably antique in style, while at the very edges of his outline she could just discern a kind of blurred pearlescent sheen. Rupert, being only nine years old, simply accepted Tom's friend at face value; and Tom himself, sinking, as was his wont, deeply and completely into this other reality, began chattering happily, just as if he were with a classmate. But Angela was aware that they were all somehow being held within that tranquil place she had described, between the past and present, experiencing the strangely beautiful harmony of rapport with the spirit world.

They crossed the road, and slowly climbed the hill to St Helen's Church. During the walk Ed opened up about the history of this magical place, and told them why the church and the green was so important to him.
'Did you know, this stretch of open downland to the south of the church, with its beautiful trees and grass field, holds a terrible secret? Not many people know about it, but before the last plague, there was a large pond at the top of St. Helen's Green which was used as a 'plague pit', disposing of the victims of the 'Black Death'. Many bodies were buried here. It has never been dug up. Sometimes, it's better to let things stay as they are. Oh look, there's the tower of the church. We're nearly there.'
They reached the church, standing isolated on a hill, in a bleak, distant spot high on the South Downs above Hove. It was quiet. The sound of the wind was whispering through the trees, their branches swinging, revealing glimpses of the tower and its narrow lancet windows.
Ed opened the small wooden gate and they followed

him through the small churchyard. The ground underfoot was hummocked with the undulations of old sunken graves. Crucifixes and mossy tombstones engraved with old inscriptions loomed in the darkness. Tom looked to his left, and spotted four crows sitting on the branches, cawing in the dark trees. They struck him suddenly as malign: black creatures which escort deceased souls from Earth to the afterlife. It was as if the birds were trying to say something, connecting the material world with the world of spirits. He began to feel uncomfortable about being here in the churchyard after all. Could this be a warning sign and should he tell his brother and sister what he felt, and return to the Manor? He looked at them, they were mesmerised by Ed's charm, and had followed him to the small wooden door, determined to enter the space beyond it. Ed turned the cast iron ring handle with both his hands and they entered the nave of the church. Tom, realising that after all his work to persuade them to come, it was too late to convince them to go back, also stepped into the ancient building.

When he closed the door behind him, he felt the cold inside the church, making him shiver. Ed beckoned Tom, Angela and Rupert to follow him to the south east corner of the chancel, where he stopped in front of a wall.

'Let me show you this monument, it belongs to my family.' Tom, Angela, and Rupert looked at the rectangular monument displaying a family carved in stone, a man and a woman and their ten children, kneeling and praying at a prayer-bench with a book open on either side.
'There are ten children displayed at a prayer-bench, but if you look closely, you can see five other children. My parents, Richard and Mary Bellingham, had five more children, but tragically they died in early childhood as a result of the Black Death. They are not forgotten either and four daughters, and one son, are represented, wearing their night gowns below where Richard and Mary kneel. Their coffins and bodies are buried in the floor below our feet.'
Angela was struck by the solemnity and strangeness of the moment. And it was curious how clearly, despite the darkness of the church, they could make out the stiff little figures on the monument, engraved into the pale stone. As she tried to give Ed's family a moment of respectful silence, Angela's attention was distracted and she looked at Ed's hand, clinging on to a small object. It looked familiar and she wondered whether it was the same little bag Tom found earlier outside the entrance of the Manor? She was about to ask him when a couple of black feathers fluttered down in front of her. She

looked up and saw four crows, sitting on the timber beams, high up in the roof shaking their black tail feathers. One sat still, observing her with its head cocked to one side. The crows moved their heads around nervously, and started making deep, rasping calls.

Just then the door opened and the black birds fled into the dark sky. Out of nowhere four girls appeared in the nave, giggling and floating above the cold stone tiled floor. Angela, Rupert, and Tom looked in amazement as the small girls moved towards the entrance, and sensed the sudden change in the atmosphere. Ed looked at the four girls who were approaching them slowly, and whispered, "My sisters are here - but they're in one of their strange moods! I didn't tell you, but they are tragically afflicted. They have always been unpredictable - some would say, mad. They're prone to fly into violent rages - attacking people, even family! I don't know what they could do to you. I think you should get out of here, quickly!"

Angela, Rupert, and Tom tried to comprehend what Ed just told them when suddenly the girls slammed the gate shut, making a loud bang. They were trapped. Ed turned to Tom and spoke rapidly, *'Tom, you've lost this little bag, filled with special marbles. Luckily I found it. Please take it back, and promise me you look after it. It was a gift from my father. My sisters are furious and are after them. But I need to tell you something important about them right now - please listen! These marbles contain the very essence of our memories, our souls - and that's why my sisters are so obsessed with them. But their fragile minds are very vulnerable to Dark forces - I fear that they're being influenced by some kind of demonic power and worse still, I'm terrified that if they get their hands on this bag again, they'll give them to the Darkness which is following them. We'll all be lost forever. You've got to take them out of here.'*

Ed ushered Angela, Rupert, and Tom to the altar and pulled away a heavy red silk curtain. Behind it was a small door built in the North wall of the church. Angela looked puzzled at the size of the door. "We can probably just squeeze ourselves through it, why is it so small?"

'It was created so the devil could escape from the church as it resided in a child's soul,' whispered Ed. *'It was driven out of the child during a baptism and somehow, had to leave the church. They believed it to be small for it to be able to house inside of a child, hence the size of the door. You're lucky it hasn't been bricked up to prevent the devil from re-entering. Listen! You've got to hurry up and leave. Once the bag's out of the church they'll stop haunting you.'*

Ed puts something in Tom's hand. *'It's a special marble, my father made it for me. Take it as a token of our friendship. It will protect you. Now go!'* He pushed Angela, Rupert, and Tom through the small door, and they ran down the hill as fast as they could, back to the Manor.
Outside the entrance they fell into the arms of their worried parents who had desperately searched the area, trying to find their children. They told their parents what happened. Guy and Isabel asked why their children had gone to the church after they were told by them and the manager not to go there. Tom apologised and said he was to blame. He explained that he persuaded his siblings to go after he conversed with the spirit of a boy who invited him to meet his sisters in the church. From the moment they entered, these sisters started to haunt them, and wanted the bag of marbles. Guy and Isabel listened in amazement and ultimately decided to leave the site, and immediately they left to bring their children to safety, far away from the church.

Back in the cottage the family talked about what had happened, and decided to cut short their stay. As it was after midnight they decided to spend the night in the cottage, and to leave early in the morning. That night, Angela had a dream. She was one of the children of Richard and Mary Bellingham, the keepers of the Hangleton Manor in the sixteenth century. She, and her siblings, were sitting in front of an open fireplace, whilst her parents were travelling to The Black Lion for a meeting with a stonemason to discuss the shipping of the stones from Lewes Priory, to be used to build a wall around the Manor. Angela felt very warm, she was sweating, and the imaginary heat of the open fireplace felt so real that it woke her up.

She opened her eyes and the first thing that sprang to her mind was Tom. Worried about him, she pulled back the duvet cover, stepped out of her bed, and quietly peeked into her brother's bedroom. Tom lay in his bed asleep, probably dreaming. At the same moment the window was flung open and a cool wind reached Angela's face. Tom woke up and looked into Angela's eyes. Reading each other's mind, they turned towards the open window and saw the face of a girl. Tom shouted. "It's one of Ed's sisters. They've found us!"

The girl floated though the open window into the room, followed by her sisters, their eyes searching the room to find their trophy. In seconds they spotted the little bag and grabbed it from the bedside table next to Tom's bed. Tom jumped up, clenched his fingers around the bag, and forcefully tried to take it from their hands. He firmly held on to it but they wouldn't have it and pushed him away. The little bag split, and Tom fell backwards. All the marbles dropped on the floor. The sound was like a hail storm hitting a window. They rolled down the old sloping floor towards the stairs. The sisters started screaming, the piercing sound was unbearable, and Angela fled down the stairs followed by bouncing marbles. Tom was stunned lying on the floor on his side. He could feel there was something in his pocket. He took it out and looked at it. It was the special marble Ed had given him just before he pushed him through the side door of the church earlier that evening. The sisters gazed jealously at the marble, which was made by their father, especially for Ed.

Tom saw someone approaching outside in the air. In a moment, the figure was floating through the window, and Tom instantly recognised him. It was Ed. The room was filled with a powerful light and energy coming from the boy's body. A bolt of light bounced against the wall, back into the room, absorbing the girls' bodies, and pushed them back through the open window into the sky. Ed left with them and Tom caught a last glimpse of his face, looking back over his shoulder. Tom held up the special marble, glinting in the darkness, so that Ed could see that he had it safe. He saw his friend's ghostly face light up in a smile as he faded into the night. Then Tom got up to lock the window and closed the curtains.

Isabel suddenly woke up, switched on the light on the bedside table, and could hear somebody crying. It was Angela. She jumped out of the bed, rushed down the narrow staircase, and ran into her room. She found her daughter hiding underneath the duvet. "Oh gosh, my poor child, you're shivering. Were you having a nightmare?" She was looking worried and gave her daughter a tight hug.
"I'm so afraid, Mum, I think I had a nightmare, it was a mix of reality and having a dream. I was in my room, and then, I don't know how, but suddenly I was in Tom's room. The sisters appeared, the bag with the marbles split, and I have a sort of idea that they vanished through the window with Ed." Angela was sobbing.
"Mum, please look under my bed. Tell me what you can see."
Isabel knelt down on the floor and looked. There were dozens of marbles underneath her daughter's bed. How on earth could so many marbles fit into a bag? What was going on here? She believed what her daughter had told her and took her upstairs.

That night, as old as she was, Angela slept in her parents' room.

The next morning the family picked up all the marbles in Angela's bedroom. Once the floors were cleared, they packed their suitcases, leaving the bag of marbles on the table.
Tom was worried about leaving the bag of marbles behind, unguarded. He discussed the problem with Angela. "The marbles didn't come from this cottage," she said. "You found them up by the Manor. I really don't think we have the right to take them away from this area. We should send them back."
"I agree, we should leave them behind. I'm sure Ed will come back and guard them in some way. It still remains a mystery where the marbles underneath your bed came from?"
They left the bag on the table, with a note asking for them to be returned to Hangleton Manor.

On the backseat of the car, Tom quietly held on to his special marble, rolling it in his fingers. He was mesmerised, looking not only at one, but five swirls. Five small children's souls, frozen in time. In his mind he could see Ed and a man, sitting down on the stone floor inside the church on top of the hill, many centuries ago. He could hear every word the man spoke to him as if Tom were there, sitting with them, and that memory was rooted inside him; a privilege granted to him by the marble, like being inside another person's life.

'If you look very closely, you will see a white shadow frozen in the gallery of time in each glass marble.' Richard told his son. 'Shadows lost in times past.'
'What are these white shadows papa? Are they ghosts?' the little boy asked his father, with curiosity and wonder.
'Yes ghosts, but these ghosts are not dark and terrible. These are the ghosts of memories, sad and preserved forever,' said his father.
'Ghosts of memories? What memories?' his son asked with wonder.
'Memories of times past,' his father smiled mysteriously, keeping the secret to himself.

Booking Three

The lost ghosts of thousands of long-forgotten old villages haunt Britain. Suddenly deserted, they have been left to fall into ruin, making way for modern progress. At the age of 32, Danni Stewart realised she wanted to travel the world. She gave up her full-time job, becoming a free-lance explorer and Instagram blogger. Her project was to visit and document abandoned villages in Britain, publishing a digital atlas of historical discoveries followed by over a hundred thousand people. She had just finished a project in Balsdean, once a hamlet northeast of Brighton built on top of a high hill, it had been taken over by the Ministry of Defence in 1939 and used for firing practice. The footage of the ghost walk, taking her followers along the old sites, was a huge hit. Something drew her back to Brighton, and without telling anyone, she booked a holiday-let just around the corner from The Black Lion pub as a base for further explorations.

Danni drove down from Redhill to Brighton via the M23, exchanging the green Surrey hills for the wildness of the sea. Yesterday she had read that a plethora of ghostly figures had been reported on this road, and the last report came from a driver who saw a man walking in front of her car, only to disappear when hit. During her journey, Danni remained vigilant, occasionally glancing sideways quickly, to look for anything odd, but she didn't detect any ghostly activity. On the A23 she passed the two Patcham pylons, a symbolic gateway to Brighton, welcoming guests, friends, strangers, and foes. On her left, surrounded by trees and houses, she saw the spire of the old All Saints church, built on a hill close to the old main road going into Brighton.

In front of the church was an old spring which used to be the source of the Wellesbourne, a stream that at times flowed towards the sea, joined by other springs. Danni followed the original route, bordered by tall trees swaying in a gentle breeze, passing a fountain filled with large sarsen stones supporting three entwined dolphins, upon which rested two basins. Danni parked her car near Pool Valley. It was only a five minute stroll to the cottage, tucked away in a hidden lane, away from the hustle and bustle. The cottage was cosy and very pretty, and to call it charming would have been an understatement. It was as if she had stepped back in time: and there was even an outside loo. It definitely suited her taste as she was an outdoor person. Matt had left a piece of paper on the table with a WiFi-password written on it, so she could update her blog. A variety of brochures, which Danni found on the kitchen table, were packed with tips about local tourist attractions and trips to nearby interesting towns like Eastbourne, Lewes, and Seaford. One of them, *Haunted Sussex*, grabbed Danni's attention. It mentioned the mysterious ruins of Tide Mills, an abandoned village tucked away between Newhaven and Seaford, where a lady in white had been seen wandering near the sea close to the spot where her child drowned during a heavy storm off the coast. In an instant, she knew why she had been drawn back and was desperate to see the remains of the village and she hoped that she might even encounter the lady in white.

It was just before sunset when she arrived at the car park. She found out there were a couple of car parks at Tide Mills, but this one would lead straight to the abandoned village. She walked down the concrete path of Mill Drove, situated between two narrow waterlogged ditches, obscured by trees and bushes. Heading towards the level crossing she heard birds chirping and jumping from one twig to another. For a moment, she stood still, looking up at the sky through the overhanging branches. Bright yellows and deep reds were burning on the horizon; and she stood hypnotised by the most beautiful sunset she had ever seen.

Once, the mouth of the river Ouse flowed down from the chalk hills in Lewes ending in Seaford, one of the main ports along the coast. The old town's fortunes had declined due to coastal sedimentation silting up its harbour, and persistent raids by French pirates. During the sixteenth century the town was burned down several times, but the people were a resourceful lot known for looting ships wrecked in the bay. They had even been known to cause ships to run aground by placing fake harbour lights on the cliffs.

Danni arrived at the level crossing and opened the gate. It was quiet, there was no soul to be seen. Across the rail track, a different world awaited her. The gate closed with a long slow metallic squeal, and she entered an area of ruins, wetlands, and creeks, complete with information panels telling visitors about the history of this mysterious place. She read that in 1761 a tidal mill was constructed and a new railway line was opened in 1864, connecting it to Newhaven and Seaford. The mill closed down in 1883 but the stubborn villagers, refusing to move, stayed in their properties. It was rumoured it used to be the home of an hospital, giving shelter to the mentally impaired from the South East, but after the Second World War broke out, all the villagers were evacuated. They never returned.

Standing on the wetlands, Danni looked over at the sea. There was a mystical faint yellow glow in the sky, the last rays of the sunset. She was surrounded by a peaceful silence, and sensed a light wind blowing over the shore, softly touching her skin. She wanted to read all about the history of this mysterious place, and walked along to the next information panel, placed in front of a flint wall. According to the panel this was the place where the local butcher, Nick Thomson and his wife Alison, used to live. One day, Alison mysteriously disappeared, and Nick was arrested after Alison's wedding band was found in a batch of freshly minced meat. Although Nick was eventually found to be innocent, her disappearance drove him mad, and he was put into the hospital close by the beach, she read. It was an old structure standing isolated on the shingle bank, and it shivered in the storm winds.

'That's quite a creepy story!' she thought.

Suddenly Danni screamed. Through the dilapidated

wall, a hand appeared, and grabbed her arm. Danni was terrified but her natural curiosity persuaded her to stay, rather than flee. Still frozen in shock, she heard a voice whisper. '*Tell him to leave now!*'
"Who? Who do I need to tell to leave?" Danni's voice was quivering.
'The butcher. Find him. Tell him to go. He can't stay here any longer.'
It was a woman's voice. She sounded agitated.
'*Tell him never, ever to return! He will understand the message.*'
She pushed Danni forcefully away, so that she fell to the ground, before vanishing between the gaps of the collapsing flint stone walls. Deeply shaken, Danni's instinct told her to get out of this place; but she was a seasoned investigative blogger and here was a perfect story. Who wanted that message given to the butcher? She immediately realised that Nick Thomson needed to be found. She was determined to find him before she left.
Danni got herself up, wiped the mud off her face, and felt a cold strong wind blowing in from the coast. The weather was changing, and the sky looked ominous.
She wanted to find Nick and followed the old flint stone walls and trackways down to the beach, passing old foundations of buildings. It was high

tide, and the waves had washed up driftwood and debris on the pebble beach. Passing an old derelict wall, she heard a noise behind her, and realised her bag must have slipped off her shoulder. Looking back, her mouth dropped open. Where she had just passed a derelict wall, there was a fully formed cottage, and not just one. There were more cottages all the way back to the railway crossing. This was very strange. All the rooms were lit up, and Danni looked puzzled, wondering how she had missed these buildings. Maybe she had hit her head when that woman grabbed her arm and she fell? She followed the path towards the cottages where men were working at the mill. The entrance gate to the school was closed but a few children were playing with a ball in the twilit courtyard.

Danni approached them and, remembering what the woman said, she asked: "Do you know where Nick Thomson lives?"

"Yes I do, he lives on the beach, Nick is a lunatic," one of the girls said.

A woman appeared from behind the school gate and approached Danni. "Can I help?"

"Yes, perhaps you can. I'm looking for Nick Thomson. Do you happen to know where he lives?"

"Yes, he resides in the Chailey Hospital opposite the tidal channel, it's a hospital for adults with mental

health issues. Nick's mind has gone completely after his wife disappeared. She's never been found. At night he opens the windows of his room and screams out her name. Years ago he was declared insane by the authorities and put into the asylum right next to the sea. They say he lives in constant fear that one day the sea will come over the shingle spit and he'll drown. There's a story in the village that one time, when he was a child, the tide came over and flooded his family's cottage. The sea water began rising up the stairs, so his dad had to carry the children out to Mill House. They found safety in the top room there, but the cottage was flooded. It must have affected him - such a horrible experience for a child. Anyway, good luck. I hope you find him."
"Thank you for your help. I'd better make my way to him."

That night, the sea level was very high, and the crashing sound of the rough waves unnerved Danni. She was walking at a safe distance from the raised pebbles when she spotted a small old wooden boat blown over the shingled spit by the strong winds. It had ended up on the beach. Staring out at the sea she wondered if whoever had been in the boat, might still be out there in the cold rough water. The sky was now pitch dark, except for the silver glow from the moon shining over the water. A white-coloured building on the coastline stood out in the darkness, reflecting the moonlight. Braving the strong gusts, she managed to move closer to the sign outside the entrance, and read the name: Chailey Hospital. It was the place where she hoped to find Nick.

Danni glanced at the building and saw someone standing behind a window. Fighting the gales, Danni managed to reach the entrance, although she was scared of what she would find behind the front door. Her mental image of what might lie inside the building was based mainly on the film “One Flew Over The Cuckoo’s Nest”. She imagined a psychiatric ward like the one in the film, overseen by a martinet nurse ruling with an iron fist, whilst empty-eyed patients shuffled along the corridors in slippers. Danni shivering at the thought of it, opened the door, and entered the cold, bleak empty hall lit with oil lamps fitted on the walls. But, instead of the sight of a martinet nurse and empty-eyed patients, there was no one there.

In front of a white wall, stood an empty reception desk with a computer screen and a keyboard. Nearby upholstered armchairs were arranged around a coffee table. Next to the reception desk was a stairwell, and rapidly Danni walked up the stairs.

Instinctively she was drawn to the second floor. She spotted a light shining at the end of the corridor, coming from one of the rooms. Danni passed several closed doors, finally stopping in front of a room with a door left open. She could hear someone sobbing. Danni peered into the room, and saw a man sitting down on his bed, his head in his hands. Tears were rolling down his cheeks, leaving traces on his skin like rain drops streaming down a window. He looked up, surprised, and stopped sobbing when Danni entered the room. She sat herself next to him. "Hi, my name is Danni. I'm looking for Nick. I was told I could find him here."
"I'm Nick. What do you want from me? You're not a nurse, are you?"
"Please, do not fear me. I'm not a nurse, but I do have a message for you. After I arrived here I met a woman, and I know it's all a bit strange but she gave me a message for you. She said that you should leave. Right now. Never ever to return."
Nick took offence. "First you parade into my room and then you're telling me to leave. I don't even know you. I'm telling you now, I'm not going anywhere!"
"I'm only trying to help you. The lady said you would understand the message?" Danni added, trying to convince him.

“I don’t care what she, or you are saying. It’s been a tough day,” Nick said. “I want to forget about what happened today. Just, leave me alone.”
Danni, instinctively adopting a soft tone, reached out a hand towards him. “I’m sorry to hear you’ve had a tough day. You can tell me what happened, if you like. I’ll listen.” It seemed to help him: she could see the tense lines on his face relaxing as he calmed down.
“I do apologise for the way I reacted, but it’s been a bad day. Nick said. He paused to gather his thoughts. “This afternoon I went for a stroll along the beach and witnessed my friend Craig retrieving a corpse from the beach. It was quite a frightening experience. I’m sure it was his wife Annie and it looked like she had drowned. She had been searching and calling out for her daughter Rose who had gone out earlier that day for a dip in the sea. The weather changed dramatically, you could feel a storm was brewing, but Annie was determined to find her daughter. She swam out into the buffeting waves, and went missing in the rough seas. I felt sorry for Craig, could feel his pain, and I realised how he must have felt having lost his wife and one of his children on the same day.”
“It must have been horrific to witness such a thing, and I feel sorry for both of you.”

A heavy silence fell in the room. After a moment, Nick seemed to forget she was there, drooping his head into his hands again to hide his face. "Is - is there anything I can do?" asked Danni, tentatively. She waited, but there was no reply. A sense of urgency began to grow on her and she stood up. "I'm so sorry, but now I've given you the message, I really have to leave. Take good care, won't you?" She thought it sounded desperately inadequate but she knew it was time for her to get out. The strangeness of her situation began to strike her.
Danni left the room, quickly walking back down the stairs. She left the asylum in a hurry, running towards the level crossing with the wind at her back. What had got into her? She had taken the advice of a woman she didn't know, and then walked into the room of a man she'd never met, a total stranger. Now, she had ended up in the middle of a storm. It was now up to him to decide what to do about the message, and all Danni wanted to do was to go back to Brighton. She reached the railway, and heard the sound of a distant horn. A train was approaching. Then a figure ran out towards her. It was a woman with wild hair, her white clothes wet through. She caught hold of Danni, putting a thin hand on her arm, her grip surprisingly strong.
'Find Rose!'

"Who are you?" Danni screamed.
'Rose is my daughter. She went out for a swim early this morning. She did not return. Bring her back to me!'
"I really don't know what you think I can do to help you. I'm so confused. I must have hit my head when I fell earlier, everything seems all mixed up. I really must go!" Danni cried in desperation.
'I'm sorry, it's just that I seem to be lost in this place and until I can find my child I cannot rest. Please, you are different, you are not of this time, I can sense that. You are not afraid, and can see things others are fearful of.'
"Really I don't know what you mean, I want to get back to my car, please let me go!"
'If you help me find my daughter Rose, I will release you.'
"Rose, you said? Are you Annie?"
'Yes, please help me find her!'
Reluctantly Danni agreed and they turned back towards the sea. The storm was raging and both struggled to keep their footing as the shingle was being washed ashore along the pathway.
"Rose, Rose, please come to your mother, come home!" Danni cried towards the sea into the howling wind. "It's no use, she will never hear us. I don't know what I'm doing!"
'It's not the strength of your voice that matters but the strength of your spirit. I know she will hear you.'
Then from the waves a figure slowly emerged, a

young girl, walking steadfastly towards them. She looked serene, her hair and clothes dry and not affected by the raging storm all around her. She was looking directly at Danni, and as she came near, she saw her mother standing beside her. Rose came close and touched her mother's face, raising her freezing hand to the freezing cheek.

She stepped back, whilst her mother stared at her. They say that eyes are the window to your soul, but hers were more like an endless tunnel of darkness, impossible to see past. Tears were welling up in her eyes and she felt a lump in her throat.

'Why did you go off into the sea, my darling? Why did you not come back to me?'

"I was afraid, I wanted to run into the sea after what I had seen. I couldn't tell you, I couldn't tell anyone."

'You can tell me now, my sweetheart, as nothing can hurt you anymore.'

"I was passing the butchers, the Thomson's, when I heard raised voices and I peered through the window and I saw a terrible thing. Mr Thomson had his butcher's knife and he was shouting at his wife and then stabbed her with the knife. She cried out and then fell to the floor. I just stood there looking in the window. I was frozen, I couldn't move. I then saw him cut off her hand and put it in the big mincer and he started turning the handle. I gasped and he looked around and saw me at the window. He started towards the door and I just ran. I looked back and saw him outside the butchers shop and I just kept running and running, and I ran into the sea and didn't stop, until I lost my footing and went under the waves."

'*We are together now and for eternity.*' said Annie.

'*In my desperation to find you I went out in a small boat, but the sea was too rough and I was also taken. I have had no rest and I haunt these ruins looking for my child but now, thanks to you,*' she said, turning to Danni, '*I can once again be reunited with my daughter.*'

Rose and Annie held each other's hand as they turned towards the sea, and ventured into the waves, Danni watching them in stunned amazement.

The storm suddenly abated, and as Danni turned back towards land, the village returned to its ruined state.

So Nick killed his wife and put her through the mincer after all, thought Danni, as she made her way back to the car; but it looks like he didn't get away with it, ending up in the asylum and losing his mind. But who was the woman who wanted Nick to leave? Could it have been his murdered wife, urging him to move on and find peace?

"I think I have the makings of a great adventure story here for my new blog!"

Deryk

We moored at the Port of Dover, once called 'the haven between the hills' by Julius Caesar. For many millennia the port had been a focus for people entering and leaving Britain. On top of the cliffs, situated next to a range of impressive old forts designed to protect the country from invasion, stood a large old castle surrounded by brick walls. Its tower guided passing ships like a solid beacon. All of us had come from the Low Countries, Brabant, Flanders, and Holland, fleeing the upcoming war between the Roman Catholics and the Protestants. Prosperous and influential immigrants had become quite big business in the last fifty years, and we were promised to be given similar rights to English citizens, once we had reached England. There were twenty of us including craftsmen, clergymen, wealthy landowners and merchants. All men had to pay a fee and take an oath of allegiance to the Crown, in order to be recognised as a member of the State, as a so called 'denizen'. Denizens were permanent residents of the Kingdom of England and shared their skills with the people, and also learned from them.
After we got off the ship we travelled into town for an evening roast in the White Horse in the old town, an inn

dating back to the reign of King Edward the Third. By the time we had finished our roast it had gone dark, and we spent the night at the inn. The following morning, the staff had prepared our riding horses and carts for the journey ahead of us, and soon we made our way into the hills of Kent and its wild flower-clad grasslands. We followed the old Roman roads and trackways along the riverbanks in the Kingdom of England.

After a month of travelling, and making new friends at the local inns, we arrived in the historic county of Sussex. It was famous for its packhorse bridges crossing rivers and streams, beautiful lakes, shady woodlands and immense open fields reaching out to the sea. At a major crossing, we decided to follow the road down south over the hill overlooking the sea. By chance, we ended up in Brighthelmstone, a small and lively town situated on the east banks of the River Wellesbourne, flowing through open country fields into the English Channel. The area next to the river was widely used by local fishermen to dry their nets and store their boats in bad weather. They had a fish market at the bottom of Great East Street, which led to the road situated south of the streets with black iron railings placed on top of cliffs bordering the beach, overlooking the sea. There was a special atmosphere in the town, something I hadn't felt in the pretty villages and towns of Kent. This place was

buzzing, it was a melting pot of all sorts of people. We went to the 'Oulde Ship Inn', a renowned meeting place for smugglers tucked away in Ship Street, where people danced and sang, encountering total strangers who, by the end of the evening, had become your best friends. And so it was that I came to meet the owner of The Cricketers, who, when he heard of my skills, offered me the opportunity to become the Landlord of his inn. I was a lucky man, and Brighthelmstone would become my base. I had fallen in love with this town. It was the place where I belonged.
The next morning came, and whether we were sober or not, the time had come to say goodbye to my friends from the Low Countries. We hugged, and kissed each other on the cheeks and lips, vowing to reunite in this very same town sometime soon, to celebrate our friendship with one of my home brewed beers once I had become a brewer. My friends and I parted until we would meet again.

In England and Scotland, ale was the staple drink, and people made small amounts of ale in their cottages. They would heat water over an open fire, and the ale was brewed in the kitchen. During the reign of King Henry VIII, ale started to give way to beer, much to the disgust of older members of society who thought it was a nasty foreign brew, harming the head and making the stomach grow. Instead, it became very popular amongst many

classes, and people drank it daily, making it one of the most favourite drinks at the time. England attracted skilled beer brewers from the continent to open dedicated brewhouses in London. Although alehouses had been known in the country for hundreds of years before that, the new beer quickly caught on in pubs and inns, giving the community even more excuse to go to a place where they could meet and have a bevvy. Soon these places became better known as their 'local'.
Before I left Liège, my father made me aware of the strict rules in England: ale and beer brewing were carried out separately, with no brewer being allowed to produce both. But after I arrived in England, I learned that ale had come to refer to any strong beer, and many ales and beers were hopped, and I found out that hops grew in Brighthelmstone on a significant scale. Commercial brewing began at inns, taverns and alehouses, and their licensing was controlled by the magistrates. The number of common brewers, who did not own pubs themselves, grew rapidly, but before I could secure a deal, a terrible thing happened.

One Summer evening, the sea was dead calm with a fog rolling in. It was humid and there was hardly any wind. I was talking and drinking with a couple of friends, sitting in front of their houses which were built under the cliffs, when I heard a yell coming from above us. Two men

had arrived by horse. They shouted at the farmers, urging them to move their cattle away from the coast, as far as they possibly could. They were shouting to anyone who could hear them. Earlier, they had spotted a large number of ships coming from the east. Some moored at Meeching and Seaford, sending boats with men to the shore. The men had fled the village of Seaford by horse to warn us.
In a rush, my friends and I left the beach, each of us running into the town shouting to people to leave their houses immediately. We knocked on every single door, urging people to follow us to the West Gate. We climbed the hills as quickly as we could, passing the chalk pit before we reached the church. The Saint Nicholas church stood on a steep hill within an old walled churchyard with burial grounds and curved lawns with trees planted either side of the paths. We climbed the main path leading to the wooden entrance gate and banged on the door. "Father Jennings, it's the people from the town of Brighthelmstone! This a cry for help, we need your help urgently. The French have arrived and there are hundreds of them!" The Vicar opened the door for us to seek shelter, and he shared his beer and bread.
From the moment I entered the majestic nave with its high arcades supported by columns and its clerestory windows tucked under the vaulted ceiling, I sensed a quiet and sacred ambience in utter silence. For centuries

people's lives were strongly connected with the church, from the beginning to the end and everything in between. People could see the sacred structure from all around, and at night a fire was lit in the square crenellated flint church tower, providing a beacon for fishermen at night. Looking north, behind the two wooden windmills with their large sails, I could see the flames dancing on top of Ditchling Beacon. This was a large neighbouring chalk hill with a steep northern face, which could be seen from quite a distance. The beacons were lit to warn everybody living in Blatchington Village, Lewes, and Rottingdean about the enemy fleets which had landed in the south, preparing themselves to fight the invaders. What were we going to do?

As we were waiting anxiously near the church, we guessed that the French fleet was slowly gliding over the water at a safe distance from the white cliffs. It was hidden in a cloud of thick coastal fog touching the sea, making it almost impossible to see from the hill and the shore.

There was a breeze coming up, blowing flurries of fog over the land. Small waves washed up on the shore as large white sails broke through the fog, and slowly the shape of the approaching deep-hulled sailing vessels became visible.

The villagers looked down from the hill. A large fleet of ships had moored in the sea with gunports in the side of each hull, their prows and sterns raised high above the waterline. Numerous pennons and light streamers adorned each ship, waving in the wind, some bearing a fleur-de-lys, and others a cross. Eight galleys were equipped with dozens of armed soldiers, and they headed towards the shore, rowing swiftly, oars creaking, and water splashing. Within minutes they reached the coast and set foot on land where they found a number of fishermen's boats.

The great ships rode hard by the shore and shot broadsides into the hills and walls of the town. The hail of cannon was so dangerous at this point that it prevented us from venturing down to fight the invaders. The soldiers lit their torches, divided themselves into eight groups, and quickly set light to the boats and houses built under the cliffs. Two other groups marched up from the Old Steine towards the town following the road going to Lewes. Soon flames could be seen rising from every house in the upper town. They had come here for one reason, to burn the place down.

In total, over fifteen hundred Frenchmen had landed and their aim was to leave a trail of death and destruction from Dover to as far as Land's End. The people living in the fisher villages were fed up with the re-incursions by the French, who had been attacking the Sussex coast since the fourteenth century.

All villagers waited outside the church of Saint Nicholas,

the faithful patron saint of sailors, merchants, thieves, brewers, and pawnbrokers, sadly surveying the illuminated town. The villagers, together with the farmers and fishermen, had gathered to oppose the expected attack. The sight became too much for us and, finally, when our anger had risen to breaking point, I shouted 'Attack!' We all ran down the hill. Before they could cause even more mayhem, we met them at North Street with vengeful resistance, using great force. We were armed with scythes, knives and bill hooks but we attacked the French invaders so vigorously that many were slain in attempting to recover their galleys, and over a hundred Frenchmen got killed or drowned in the sea.
We all stood on top of the cliffs watching the blaze. The flames were everywhere, and I could feel the heat coming from the flames, scorching my skin. Through the smoke I looked at the town: Brighthelmstone was burned down to the ground, and people's eyes were brimmed with tears. In our midst stood the Vicar of the Saint Nicholas church, William Jennings, who praised our bold behaviour during this devastating night. We'd lost our houses, all our belongings, and had nowhere to stay. The vicar, as kind as he was, said to follow him back to the church where he would open the door to us to spend the night. At least we had a roof over our head, and the church would provide food and drink, but our biggest worry was, would the town be able to rise from the ashes?

Booking Four

Marilyn was a gorgeous, self-sufficient, confident woman in her prime. She was a much loved counsellor, seeing clients in Brighton and London. Consumed by wanderlust at the tender age of 18, she left her family home in East Sussex and became an au-pair in Antwerp. After she travelled back to the UK, she married a guy named Michael, and became an Image Consultant within the fashion and music industry in London. After several years, she discovered that she preferred female company and headed down south where she found a spacious flat in Hove and retrained as a therapist. In search of the person she wanted to marry and spend the rest of her life with, she made many new friends, and maintained their friendships by meeting up for lunch, dinner, or a drink in town. Her friends enjoyed her charm as she was genuinely interested in people, wanting to get to know you, and making them feel the most special person in the world.

It was Friday morning, Matt had just made himself a cup of tea when his phone pinged.

He looked at the screen, it was a message from his friend Marilyn whom, he hadn't heard from lately.

Hi darling. I hope you're well? I'm sorry I haven't been in touch. Life's been very hectic! I've met somebody new, but I have to vacate my flat. If possible could I rent that lovely cottage of yours whilst I'm looking for a new flat? It will only be for a week, or so. Let's meet up one morning next week? Missing you xxxxx

After he took a sip of tea, he texted her back.
Hi, Lucky you, I hope you're happy, and fingers crossed you'll find a new place soon. The cottage is vacant for the next 3 weeks. I'm around Monday or Tuesday. Where do you want to meet? xxx

Hi, that's fab! Please book us in for the full period. I can do next Monday. Shall we meet around 11:00 am at St Nicholas Rest Garden? Lots of love xxxxx

I've booked you in. Next Monday at 11:00 am is fine. It's in the diary. Looking forward to seeing you then xxx

The last time they met was when she was in a relationship with Holly. She had invited him to a dinner party in her period basement flat at Lansdowne Place. The evening started with talks about their peculiar travels to the Salem's Witch Museum which told the true story behind the Salem witch trials of 1692; and to the hill of crosses in Lithuania, an old mound hunched under the weight of thousands of crosses, the exact origins of which remain a mystery to this day. Matt told them about his visits to the remote necropolis in the Valley of the Kings in Egypt with hidden tombs beneath the desert; and to the Père Lachaise Cemetery in Paris, a city by itself, where visitors have encountered ghosts along its shaded cobblestone paths. Gradually the subject changed from travelling to paranormal experiences, and ghost sightings.

After the other guest had left and over a glass of wine, Marilyn told Matt she always felt scared when Holly was not around. Holly was a Police Constable and worked a lot of night shifts, patrolling West Street and the seafront in particular. Therefore, most evenings Marilyn spent her time alone in the flat. Matt remembered her telling him: "It feels like I'm being watched all the time. I can feel a presence whenever I'm by myself, it's driving me crazy. One evening I was watching a TV show, *Is there life after death?* - it was probably not the best programme to watch by myself." That evening, she told him, she felt cold and lonely, and her eye caught something moving near the sofa. Nervously she glanced at the

sofa and at that moment some petals from the lilies in the vase standing next to it dropped onto the floor. Her unease grew. She was adamant she'd seen someone, a boy. Determined to find him she left the room and peeked into the bedroom but there was no one there. She opened the door of the bathroom, and it was empty, as if he had managed to escape. She heard a noise. It came from the lounge. Immediately she dashed back and found the vase on the floor - broken, surrounded by lilies scattered all over the carpet. Was it her imagination or was it due to the bottle of wine she had drunk? Then she could hear somebody walking down the steps outside her flat. She locked herself into the bathroom, her hands shaking as she heard the person stop outside the front door. Someone inserted a key into the lock, and pushed down the door handle. Marilyn was holding her breath.
"Hi hun, I'm home." Holly stepped into the hallway and put her keys on the console table. Marilyn flushed the toilet, walked into the hallway, relieved to see Holly had returned home early.
Another evening Marilyn came back from a night out with her colleagues. She poured herself a glass of wine, sat down on the sofa, and looked at the wall opposite. She noticed one of the three pictures above the dining table was crooked. She wondered

whether Holly had moved it? Then other strange things happened. Once she came back from work to find all the chairs lined up against the wall. Another day she grabbed a snack from the kitchen, but when she walked back to the corridor the door mat had been flicked over. Marilyn felt uneasy at first, but later she grew accustomed it. These inexplicable events didn't occur when Holly was around, or when friends came over for dinner. It only occurred when she was by herself. Holly didn't believe her stories and she wondered whether she was going mad.

In the week following the dinner party Marilyn went to see Beth, her local hairdresser, and told her about the mysterious things which had been happening at her flat. Beth used to live with her parents on the ground floor, just above Marilyn's flat, and she told her that the flat was previously occupied by a man and a woman who were in a troubled relationship. One of the neighbours told Beth that she believed the man kept the woman locked up in the flat after she had given birth to their son. Nobody ever saw the woman but sometimes they could hear someone crying.
"The years went by," Beth told Marilyn," and neighbours living next door to the couple wondered what was going on as they hadn't seen the woman

for ages. One day the man told my mother he was moving out after he had lost his job, and was no longer able to afford the rent."

Gradually, as Beth worked on Marilyn's hair, the story unfolded. She told her that the landlord contracted a local building company to refurbish the basement flat. The builders made the acquaintance of the neighbours, and found out about stories of the mysterious disappearance of the woman and a child, suspecting something awful may have happened there. The builders said they'd been in the flat and didn't see anything unusual, but they would keep their eyes open.

The works were supposed to be completed within three months but it took longer than anticipated, and the landlord extended their contract by another month. One morning a Police van arrived and two Police Constables went into the basement, using the separate entrance via steps that led down from the footway above. Another Police car arrived, followed by an ambulance. The neighbours were very worried, thinking that one of the builders had been injured. Less than an hour passed when two PC's walked up the steps carrying something that looked like two body bags. The neighbours stood on the pavement, talking to each other, and were convinced the raid must be in connection with the

disappearance of the woman.
A few weeks later, the local newspaper revealed that the autopsy found evidence that the woman who had lived in the basement had been killed by a blow and buried in the concrete floor of the bathroom. The newspaper reports speculated that a brutal murder had taken place, even that the victim had been buried alive.
"What a terrible thing to do, don't you think?" Beth said.
Marilyn's hair was standing up on end. "It's horrific, Beth! I feel very frightened. The thought of this gruesome event happening in my flat, it's just too much! I can even feel and imagine the memory of it. I'm really sorry, but I think I have to go. Just let me know how much I owe you and I'll pay you later."
Marilyn left, phoned her GP, and explained what happened. She was signed off sick for six weeks, prescribed anti-depressants, and never saw the boy-child again.
Unfortunately, Holly could not deal with what she called Marilyn's 'so called' paranoia, especially as Marilyn was now saying she had seen a small boy in her flat, Holly thought Marilyn was getting broody. Holly definitely did not want a family, she took this as her cue to move out. Marilyn turned to her friend Matt for sympathetic advice and told him about the

history of the flat and the reason for her break-up with Holly.
Marilyn, unable to live by herself, met Aysha, and soon Aysha moved in permanently. After a couple of months she received a letter from the landlord with the request to vacate the property as she was going to put it up for sale. Marilyn had to hunt for a new flat and it was at this point that Matt kindly offered her to stay in the cottage for three weeks.

It was early Monday morning and Matt entered the St Nicholas Rest Garden through the stone archway. Laid out back in 1840 as an extension cemetery for St Nicholas church, used for burials, it was now a green and leafy breathing space not far from the busy shops of Western Road. The garden was almost deserted when he followed the pathway around the large Victorian tombs, which formed a terrace on the north side of the graveyard. Their fourteen bays were designed in a Tudor-Gothic style, as if they were entrances to the vaults. Matt stopped in front of them and observed each of the vaults, his attention taken by one in particular, tempted to reach and touch its door. Out of all the gates only the second door on the left appeared to be made out of wood. Matt tapped the wooden surface to check whether it was real or fake. To his surprise he heard

a rattling noise coming from inside the vault. It was the sound of clanging metal, as if a heavy chain were being removed. The door slowly creaked open and a man appeared, dressed in a green and yellow suit, holding a large shovel. "Good morning. I'm just getting all my tools ready. It's a perfect day for a Spring clean in the garden, isn't it?" he said smiling.
"I'm sure it is," Matt said relieved, "Well, have a good day."
He walked past the man, and spotted Marilyn sitting down on a wooden bench under a large broad-leaved tree with overlapping crowns, and sunlight penetrating through the branches. They spotted each other at the same moment, and Marilyn stood up from the bench, stretching out her arms.
"Hello, dearest. How are you?"
"I'm good, darling. It's been too long! You don't look a day older." Matt gave her a peck on the cheek.
"How are you?"
"I'm fine, thank you. It's good to see you."
"Let's sit down and you can tell me the reason why we're meeting today."
"We're not here to talk here about my new 'flame', we've only just started dating, and I'll tell you more about her another time, I promise. The reason why we're here is, well, I honestly, I don't know where to start. I've never been very open about my family,

have I?"
"Perhaps you haven't, but everybody is entitled to a little bit of privacy."
"Yes, I agree. Well, please let me try to explain a little bit more about my family, as I think that's the main reason why we're here. Something odd has happened recently and it's connected with the flat I live in, hence I texted you. Do you happen to remember what I told you about that awful thing that happened to the woman who used to live there?"
"Do you mean the woman they found in the bathroom?"
"Spot on. Well, recently I've not been sleeping very well. I was getting those recurring visions again about the small boy I've seen before in the flat, but this time, it looked like he has, somehow, matured. He has dark hair and wears black clothes, and tries to talk to me. I thought it may be related to whatever happened in my flat. The frustrating thing is that I can't seem to understand what he's trying to say. The whole situation has kept me awake for many nights, I keep on seeing the little boy, and my work has been suffering badly. In the end I went to see the Doctor again, and they've given me some medication and advised me to rest."
Marilyn took a deep breath, and continued. "Last

week my auntie Bev contacted me, and she asked me to meet up for lunch at the Farm Tavern. They allocated us a table in the cosy corner next to the bay window, and I must say, we had the most delicious roast ever. I would highly recommend it. Now, let me explain what we discussed. Auntie Bev, my mother's sister, told me a lot about my childhood that I seemed to have blocked out, but my aunt said it was now time that I remembered.

"She told me my mother never showed any affection to me or my sister and abandoned us when I was very young, wanting to make a new start with her lover Martin Collins. As a result my sister and I were sent to a residential home in Hove. My real father had left some while before, off to sea, never to return. The women were very kind and caring, they truly looked after us. My aunt could only take one of us in and she chose me, whilst my sister was sent to a family house in Alfriston.

"Some years later my aunt found out my mother's fiancée, Martin Collins, had been arrested and imprisoned for murder. My aunt never told me this until now, and for some unexplained reason, I opened up to her about my ghost-sightings of the boy in my flat. I told her that Holly wanted to leave me as she thought I wanted to start a family, and soon after she had left the sightings stopped.

Perhaps she was right and I did want to become a mother, without realising it. Immediately my aunt put her cutlery down and looked straight into my eyes. 'The boy who appears in your vision, is there anything else you can remember other than he had dark hair and was wearing black clothes?'
"I told her I remembered a staircase, the boy was sitting on the bottom step holding a black and white photograph of a woman, and she looked somehow familiar. I asked whether she thought the lady in the picture could be my mother? My aunt didn't answer or say anything more about it and we finished our lunch."
Marilyn opened her handbag, took a tissue and wiped the tears from her cheeks. She took a deep breath, calmed herself down, and put back a smile on her face, staring at the cherry trees. Their beautiful blossoming pink flowers stood as the backdrop of the facade of the burial vaults.
"Last Wednesday I told Beth, my hairdresser, about what happened to my mother's fiancé, Martin Collins and how he was arrested. Beth looked at me in an odd way, and said the gentleman of the couple with the child who used to live in my flat, was also called Martin. She wondered what happened to their son Tony.
"Darling, it was like my head was hit by a bolt of

white lightning. Instantly I remembered the word I had seen the boy was trying to speak, 'Tony'! I phoned the Police regarding the arrest of Martin Collins, told them about what happened in my flat, and, guess what? When the police were called in after that renovation work revealed suspicious activity in the bathroom, they had already received an anonymous tip-off about the unexplained disappearance of Jane and her son Tony. That's why they were so quick to send a couple of police constables to the basement flat.

"After they had found the remains of his partner, concreted in the bathroom floor, they questioned Martin, and in tears, he confessed he had murdered his partner unintentionally. He claimed it all happened by accident and he was terrified that if he were observed carrying her body up the stairs, he would look like a murderer.

"I can't imagine why Martin Collins thought like that! When I heard the story, I kept wondering if he was so innocent, why not just phone for an ambulance? But then I remembered what Beth had said, that the poor woman was never seen, but only heard crying. I think the man was guilty of domestic abuse for years and was afraid it would all come out. He knew he had already caused her untold suffering.

"He came up with the plan to hide her body in the basement flat, bought some cement, and created a raised bathroom. Once the concrete had set, he placed her body in it, and tiled over it so nobody would ever find her. The Police also confirmed they found a second body, a boy, approximately six years old. Martin confessed the remains were those of their son Tony, who died of natural causes. He told them that on the same morning, Jane found their dead child and accused Martin of killing him, insisting she was like a mad woman, hitting and shouting at him, asking if he had done it. He said he didn't, but she kept on accusing him of the murder of their child. Pushing her away, she slipped, fell backwards, and hit her head on the floor. Martin knelt down, took her arm, but he felt no pulse. She was dead and he buried her and their child in concrete to conceal what happened."
Marilyn looked at Matt, devastated, her eyes welling up. "When I was a child I remembered my mother's name was Jane. It feels weird that, on separate occasions, my mother and I have been living in the same flat, the same space, I honestly didn't have a clue. Looking back now, the signs were clearly there. It was me who could see the little boy, hear him crying, somebody who was trying to connect with me, the spirit of my little brother, Tony."

A light wind blew through the garden, the leaves rustled in the oak tree, causing the flowers to release a beautiful and intense fragrance.
"It's all very sad," Marilyn said. "I've spent the last few days going over and over it all in my head. I could hardly think straight and in the end, I knew I needed someone to talk to. I hope you don't mind my unloading all this on you, Matt?"
Matt put his hand on her shoulder. "Come on, love. We've been friends for ages. You can tell me anything."
They sat in silence for a while and gradually, Marilyn's face calmed and cleared. After a while, she looked up at the cherry blossom. "You know," she said, "I've lived here most of my life - but it's the first time I've been to this garden. It's such a tranquil place, and oh so pretty, isn't it?"
"Yes, it is. What was it that drew you here?"
"One of my friends, who came to visit me last week, recommended I should go here. He said when you take in the beauty of the garden it eases the mind. Well, I must say, it certainly has. He also recommended visiting St Ann's Well gardens, it's just around the corner from where I live. I may as well make the most of it whilst the weather is nice."
"I'm sure it will do you some good, as you said. Make the most of it."

"Now I've explained everything, I hope you understand why I need to move out of that flat, and I really appreciate your offer to stay in the cottage for the next couple of weeks, it will really help me out. Aysha will be so happy, and I can clean the place as well and tidy it up for you."
"Anytime. I'll text you the code for the keypad lock."

After they got up off the wooden memorial bench, Marilyn and Matt walked through the park looking at the tomb stones. Many of the inscriptions had become worn beyond recognition, but some were still readable. They stopped in front of one of the graves and looked at the headstone.

To the memory of Jane & Anthony Collins of Hove who passed away on the morning of 6th August 1967.

Marilyn was staring at the headstone, her face pale, just standing there. Gradually, the colour came back to her face, she turned to Matt, and took his hands: "I think I'm in shock, darling. This can't be true. I think we should go."
Just before Marilyn turned to leave, Matt noticed a crumpled up piece of glossy paper near the headstone. He stooped and picked it up, unfolding and smoothing it out as he did so. Silently, he

handed it to Marilyn. Confused, she looked at the item he had given her. She was holding a black and white photograph of a boy standing next to a lady whose face looked very familiar. It was the same picture the boy had been holding in her visions. Standing in shock, Marilyn's hands let the picture fall, fluttering back down onto Jane and Tony's grave.
"If you want we can go to your flat, get your essentials, and I'll take you over to the cottage right now. I've parked my car just around the corner," said Matt, after watching Marilyn in concern. He could see that this last shock was simply too much for her and she looked as though she might buckle at the knees.
"That would be a good idea;" said Marilyn numbly. "Thank you, you're a real treasure."

Marilyn and Aysha spent a couple weeks in Black Lion Cottage, viewing one flat after another. They finally took a liking to a second floor apartment at Wick Hall, built in the 1930s on the ancient site of the old Wick Manor. The hill was locally known as Furze Hill. It was an Art Deco complex, a residence of unique charm, moments away from the green open spaces of St Ann's Well Gardens, and they could move in immediately.
Aysha was very excited: "I love the flat, it's a

perfect location, and so close to where we live now. Shall we take it?"
"It's a lovely flat, but a little bit expensive."
"Ok. Let's talk about it tonight," said Aysha looking at the clock. "I'm afraid I have to go back to work now."
"Ok, you'd better go, otherwise you'll be late. We've viewed so many flats this week, but I do like this flat. I'm going for a stroll in the park. I'll see you tonight."
They kissed goodbye and Marilyn walked to St Ann's Well Gardens, a beautiful park with winding pathways, beds of aromatic shrubs, a fish pond with water lilies. There was even a little waterfall with birds drinking and sprinkling their feathers. She always had sensed something special and sacred about the place, and recently she had read there was an ancient spring here, which used to attract lots of people to drink its water with their allegedly healing powers.
Wandering through the gardens, she entered a small space shielded by a ring of trees, with steps going down to a bricked circle with wooden benches, surrounding a pretty wishing well with its characteristic shingled roof. A woman with blonde hair and fair skin passed the bricked and wooden well, and when she noticed Marilyn approaching,

she quickly turned onto the path between the chestnut trees and ferns, seeming to vanish into thin air near the rose garden. Marilyn saw something glittering in the sunlight on the edge of the well. Someone had left behind a charming silver scroll holder with repoussé motifs, decorated with foliage and flowers. Marilyn picked it up and opened it. Inside she found a beautiful old parchment scroll, entitled '*The Legend of St Ann's well*', *written by Alfred, in memory of my daughter Annefrida.*
Intrigued, she sat down on one of the wooden benches, and started to read the story.

In the sixteenth century, built on top of Wick Hill, stood the Manor of Wick, in the middle a narrow band of fields with shrubs of yellow flowering gorse stretching from the sea, meeting the boundary of Preston Manor in the north. In the manor lived a family with their young and beautiful daughter, Annefrida, who wanted to travel the seas and discover exotic places all over the world. She had been introduced to the handsome nobleman Wolnoth, fell deeply in love, and their marriage was arranged to take place on his return from the wars on sea.
The day arrived when she expected him to come home, and the wedding preparations were nearly completed. The sunset came, but still there was no sign of Wolnoth. Haunted by the most terrible fears, Annefrida retired

silently to her room.
The same night, a messenger came to the Manor with some horrific news. They had found the body of Wolnoth, covered in blood, in the hills west of Brighthelmstone, about half-a-mile from the coast, and it looked like he had been cruelly murdered.
Three days later, the brave and faithful Wolnoth was buried. A marble cross was placed at the head of the grave, and the contiguous ground was blessed by the Bishop of St Nicholas Church. When Annefrida reached the sacred enclosure, and saw the marble cross, she started sobbing, threw herself upon the grave, and burst into tears. Annefrida cried, for hours, her tears flowing continuously, and every day, the poor Annefrida returned to the graveyard, spending her time crying, grieving the loss of Wolnoth.
A group of little bright-haired children of the shepherds who lived close by Wick Hill, watched out for Annefrida on a daily basis, and brought her wild flowers to place on the grave. But one day, a little child came up to her, and said: "Don't cry, dear lady. When you're sad, it makes us sad, and seeing you cry, every day, makes us cry too."
Annefrida's tears ceased for a moment as she listened to the child, she tilted her head, smiled, and kissed the little one.
"Yes, dear child, what you just said is so true, seeing sad people cry, makes other people cry, and from now on I

will try not to cry and will help you and your little friends all to be good."

One night, Annefrida had a haunting dream in which she thought she heard a voice, her dear Wolnoth was calling out to her, 'Annefrida, my beloved one,' said Wolnoth, 'I have seen your love and your sorrows, and how you daily watered my grave with tears. It must be hard, not having me with you, we were separated so soon, before we even got married. I'm thinking of you, and for me it's hard too not having you around me, but we will see each other one day, and I will propose to you once more to become my beloved wife, but till then, my loved one, for my sake and for your own, and for the sakes of those who love you on earth, let your grief and sorrow go, and let me sleep. Try to keep it in your faithful loving heart, let it not become a burden to others. Help those little children, help them all you can, and put a smile on their faces. The tears you have shed on my grave shall not be lost, as for where they fell, a spring shall rise and flow for evermore.'

The following day, Annefrida's parents, at her persuasion and pleasing their dear child, went with her to see if the spring had really risen on the hill. Annefrida felt in her own mind that her dream was all so true and real, and was quite sure that she would see water welling out of the ground. Annefrida was very silent, but as they

approached the spot they saw the children standing and looking at something, and at once she knew that her dream was fulfilled. When the little ones saw her coming, they ran to her. "Lady Annefrida, Lady Annefrida, the ground is crying, come and look."
"Is it, little ones?" she said, taking her little favourite's hand. She went to the spot, and saw a clear spring bubbling out of the mound just above the head of Wolnoth's grave, covered with lovely wild flowers. Annefrida vowed that her life should be wholly devoted to the good of others. On rising, she turned to the little children and kissed them all. The little girl kissed her in return, and looked into her eyes.
"Dear Lady, are you one of the saints the good Bishop tells us of? You must be. May we call you Saint Ann, and may we call this place St Ann's well?"
"Yes, my child, you may if you like, but I am not a saint, but perhaps if we are good we all may be some day."
That day, when she returned home, Annefrida begged her father to write down her story, which he did on a parchment roll, placing it in a silver scroll holder, and gave it to his daughter.
Faithfully, Annefrida kept her vow and was beloved and revered by all, but she became frail, and those who knew her, witnessed that she was fading away. One morning , exactly three years after Wolnoth's death, she was found dead in her bed, looking calm and peaceful. They buried

her with the silver scroll holder, being placed in her coffin as she desired, beside her Wolnoth.
The Bishop of St Nicholas, when performing the funeral rites said: 'Truly our departed one is now a Saint in Heaven, and henceforth let her be known amongst you as St Ann, and the holy well on Wick Hill beyond, the offspring of her tears, as St Ann's Well.'

In memory of my beautiful daughter Annefrida.

Your father,

Alfred

Marilyn was sitting next to the well, holding the letter in her hands, and when a tear rolled down her face she could hear laughter and singing nearby, and she stared over towards the rose garden. At the end of the path, between the chestnut trees and ferns, she saw a woman with blonde hair and a small group of children, happily dancing in a circle. Then she knew that her own ghosts were now laid to rest, and moving to the flat near St Ann's Well was the right thing to do. It would be a place for her to visit and sit in quiet reflection and find her own healing.

Deryk

The following morning I looked through the Gothic style window. The first rays of sunshine were breaking through the dark sky, and I opened the wooden gate of the church where the people had taken shelter after the violent raid. We descended the hill through the graveyard, and once we crossed North Street we arrived in a literal ghost town. The walls of the wooden houses had crumbled, and in their place stood thick beams of wood, blackened, and charred from where the flames had licked at them. The foundations were still smoking as I manoeuvred myself through the rubble. Black dust hung in the air, smelling of smouldering wood. I put my hat in front of my mouth, preventing lingering smoke from entering my lungs, and walked around the remains of my old house. Nothing had escaped the fire. Glass littered the floor where the windows had broken and the metal base of the grand wrought iron chandelier lay blackened and twisted on the ground. Finally I found what I was looking for, covered in grey ashes: my iron money box.
It was a devastating sight; the town was almost completely destroyed. Only the church, ironically made from French Caens stone, stood tall, and it would continue to guard over Brighthelmstone whilst it was

being rebuilt along the visible lines of the original streets. Plots of land had become available through the Crown's tenants-in-chiefs, which were offered to the villagers, and I took the opportunity to rent one of the plots. I learned that a tenant did not own the land, I held it in return for specified services, and had to swear homage and fealty to the King, who in turn, promised to protect us. Fortunately the coins in my iron money box had withstood the fires, and with the money, I was able to rent a substantial plot of land to build my dream, a brewery and an inn to serve my beer. I was lucky my father had given me the knowledge and the money to become a brewer, as only a few people practised this profession.

Many builders and carpenters who lived in nearby villages were recruited to rebuild the town, working hard from dawn till dusk. New cottages were built with walls made from wooden frames filled with brick, flint and pebbles, and tiled roofs, to reduce the impact of any future fires. The builders I hired made steady progress, and soon I opened the brewery and inn, welcoming my guests. It was a large three storey high structure with cellars, arches supporting the ceiling, and a large kettle surrounded by a brick circle which was heated from beneath to boil the beer. Below the ground, they had dug a deep well, catching the fresh groundwater flowing through the pores of layers of rock, the main ingredient to make beer, and in the cellars I stored sacks overflowing

with grain, barley, and hops.
Like most brewers, I produced enough beer during the winter to last through the summer, and stored it in underground cellars to protect it from the summer's heat. Once the beer was brewed, I would put it into oak barrels and let them age for a couple of months before pouring it into hand-blown thick dark glass bottles, capping them with corks, strapped with wire.
The top of the roof of the brewery was represented by a copper black lion weather vane with a brave gilded tail and a flowing mane that glittered in the sun. I had brought the weathervane with me from Flanders, and many people who visited, asked me about the origins of the name of the brewery. The heraldry of lions was well known in England for centuries - King Richard I was known as 'the Lionheart' due to his skill as a warrior. Many countries incorporated the lion in their coat of arms in their flags and shields, and the black lion became the symbol of Flanders, the ruler of the animal kingdom. At the time Black Lion Street was just a muddy road with a shoemaker, an artisan, and a wool maker, with areas of open land between the houses where I grew hops for the brewery and hemp for the rope-makers.
Soon the inn became very popular amongst locals, merchants from overseas, and smugglers alike. Merchants, who visited from the Continent, kept me informed about the situation in Flanders, and

unfortunately, it wasn't very good. They told me the situation was very tense, and if nothing would diffuse it, it could escalate leading to people being harmed or even killed, potentially causing a war between the churches and the kings.

The crossing to England had been a lucky escape, and I had high hopes the situation down here would remain stable. But one morning, in one of his palaces in London, King Edward VI became very ill, and soon this news spread to the rest of the country. If Edward VI happened to pass away, his sister Mary would ascend the throne and I would be facing a dark and turbulent future. She was a devout Roman Catholic, and if she were to become Queen, this would enrage many Protestants and everything would change. My gut feeling told me that I needed to take precautions and find someone to run the brewery in case the future cast a dark shadow over us.

Booking Five

Kay was born in Brixton, which had become one of the most vibrant neighbourhoods in South London. After a few years of extensive studies, she qualified as a teacher, and finally got the chance to get her own classroom delivering fun lessons to a room full of children. Around the same time the Brixton Pound was established, a local bartering currency. Passionate about her local community, she spent her Saturday afternoons working as a volunteer at Transition Town Brixton. She helped them launch an electronic version of the same currency where users can pay for services by text message. Kay got to work with Wayne, a friendly and handsome local landscape gardener offering help to young long-term unemployed people. Spending more time together than with other friends, they became romantically involved, and Kay moved from her parent's house into Wayne's flat. One day, Kay surprised Wayne with a mini-break in his hometown Brighton to spend a dirty-weekend away in the Black Lion Cottage.

It was a warm and sunny morning and Wayne and

Kay were having breakfast on the patio of the cottage. Kay tucked into the soft and creamy scrambled eggs. "It's a lovely cosy place, isn't it? I love the black wrought iron tee hinges on the doors, and the old wooden indoor shutters. It's a quaint old cottage but also a bit creepy."
"It gives me the creeps too," said Wayne. "This morning I read an interesting piece in this local newspaper, it was about medieval England. The pub next door is one of the oldest in East Sussex, famous for the sightings of brewer Deryk Carver, and they mentioned a couple of other nearby watering holes. A bit further afield there's the Mermaid Inn in Rye where a ghost of a maid is said to be present in the inn."
"Poor thing!" snorted Kay, a forkful of scrambled egg paused midway to her mouth. "Imagine having nothing better to do in the Afterlife than haunting your old job!"
"Ah, but she had a reason!" said Wayne. "Apparently she was the mistress of one of the smugglers of the Hawkhurst Gang, and was killed by his fellow gang members as they feared she knew too much and would expose them. The men have been seen dancing and carousing until the drinks run out."
"And when the drinks run out they sleep it off, I suppose?" said Kay drily.

Wayne laughed, but carried on quoting from the newspaper in his hand. "Listen, this is so interesting. In Alfriston stands the Star Inn, with a number of wooden figures looking down on travellers. It's where a mysterious smuggling gang used the inn as a base, and their leader disappeared after a huge storm. Every time it storms, guests were left terrified after seeing the sight of a man dressed in a night shirt with frilled cuffs, kneeling down in front of the open fire, his eyes gouged out."
Kay put her fork down. "There's no way I'll be setting foot in that place. The man has been violently executed, and his poor spirit is still there!"
"Come on, it's only one and a half hours by bus." Wayne said teasingly.
"Let's do something else instead, something to lift up our spirits. Let's go shopping in Western Road."
"Sure, if you prefer. Shall we hire one of the BTN bikes? There's a hub just around the corner. We could explore a bit more of Brighton and Hove?" Wayne suggested.
"That sounds like a plan, babe. Let's go for a ride."
They finished their breakfast, walked through Prince Albert Street to the hub at the Town Hall, and unlocked the turquoise-coloured smart bikes. Within seconds they were on their bikes and cycling on the dedicated cycle path along the seafront,

passing the impressive Old Ship Hotel dating back to the sixteenth century, the historic and luxurious Victorian hotel The Grand, and the delightful octagonal bandstand with its eight cast iron arches infilled with delicate screens. After some window-shopping and lunch, they pushed on towards the Seven Dials. As they were waiting at the traffic lights next to the Mad Hatter cafe, Wayne laughed. "I do miss Brighton but there's one thing I don't miss - its hills!"

Kay looked to her left up a tree-lined road of Victorian properties and elegant balconies fronting curved bay windows. The sign read *Montpelier Road*, and it was situated on a steep hill.

"I agree with you on that one, it is very hilly indeed," she said, laughing too. "Do you fancy a walk? We could leave the bikes behind outside Waitrose and walk up this beautiful road. According to the map it leads to the Seven Dials."

A cool breeze was coming from the sea and Kay wrapped her scarf a little bit tighter around her neck. Her eye was caught by a man with a straw hat, standing across the road, staring at her. Kay was wondering why he was looking so intently at her, when a gust blew the scarf into her face. Involuntary, she made a sudden movement and removed the scarf from her head. When she looked back, she

noticed the man had disappeared. Wayne looked at the expression on Kay's face. She looked confused.
"Hun, are you ok?"
"Just seconds ago, I saw a man with a straw hat across the road, staring at me."
"You didn't flirt with him, did you?"
Kay gave him a withering look, then smiled. "You little tease!," poking Wayne in the stomach. "Well, he just spookily disappeared. I guess I just might have scared him off."

After they had locked up their bicycles, they walked up Montpelier Road, and saw a small group of people gathered outside a cream-coloured Victorian basement flat, admiring the stylish architecture.
"Laissez-moi prendre une photo de ce très bel appartement," one of the ladies of the group said.
As Kay's mother was French, she was raised bilingually, and therefore understood what the lady said. She totally agreed with her: it was a very beautiful flat. It looked like a postcard. No wonder the lady wanted to take a picture of it. The four storey house had a terraced front garden with sweet-scented yellow daffodils and purple lavender, green shrubs, and an almond tree providing shade to the basement flat.The red brick stairs led to a black iron gate with a porch and a front door, and behind the

almond tree you could see two sash windows with yellow wooden shutters. After the group had admired the beautiful entrance and colourful garden, and the lady had taken a picture, the tourists continued their walk.

"Look!" Wayne pointed at the gate, "It's open. Shall we have a peek?"

"We can't do that. It's not our house."

"Ah, come on, it will be interesting."

"No, I don't really want to see." Kay was embarrassed by his insistence.

"I know, but I would like to have a look down there. It's an old Victorian property. This part would have been the servants' area. I could knock on the door and ask the occupant to show us around. Please?" Wayne begged Kay. "I know it's the wrong thing to do, but I feel compelled to go in. There's something about this place."

Kay flounced off as Wayne walked down to the basement, turning to stare back at him with her furious black eyes. "Right, that's it! I'm heading over to Waitrose to get some snacks. You know where to find me when you're done."

Wayne walked slowly down the narrow steps. He found the house strangely enchanting. Perhaps he was inspired by the admiration of that group of tourists looking at the pretty little garden, perhaps it was something about the building itself, but it seemed imperative that he take a look inside. He saw that the wall around the door was covered with overgrown hanging branches of ivy, as if to warn him off, and gently he pulled them away. Now he could see the door properly and noticed that someone had left a long silver key in the lock of the front door. At first he hesitated, but curious to find out what was behind it, he turned the key and the door opened with a creaking noise. He walked into the long corridor. It had terracotta-style tiles on the floor, white walls and on the right, an empty wooden coat stand. Outside he heard the wind rustling through the tree and, with a bang, the front door slammed shut behind him. Wayne felt he was trapped: the noise caused his heart to pump violently in a sudden flood of anxiety. His body was trembling and he had a sense of 'butterflies' in his stomach. There was only one entrance, and that also meant there was only one exit behind him. Wayne's first impulse was to rush back to find Kay, but he stopped short when he heard somebody shuffling behind the closed door.

"Hello?" His voice was quivering. "Anyone there?" There was no response. He put his ear against the door. The sound had stopped, but Wayne was sure there was somebody outside. He pushed down the

door handle, noticing thankfully that the key had not been turned in the lock. He peeked into the porch and, to his relief, saw there was no one there, but now the coal cellar door opposite was ajar. Wayne peered around the cellar door. The steps leading down seemed to vanish into the pitch dark space built deep below the passages. Next to the door he spotted a torch, switched it on, pushed the coal cellar door wide open, walking down the stone steps. He hardly knew why he felt compelled to investigate somebody else's coal cellar.
Suddenly he heard something, and stopped. The torch was old and dim, its weak battery casting a shaky beam onto the steps ahead. He shone his torch into the dark, and to his horror he saw something moving. In the flickering light of his torch, a pair of eyes was staring at him. His heart rate elevated rapidly, adrenaline pumping at high speed throughout his body: and then it went dark. The torch had stopped working. Wayne shook it, tried to make it work again, but nothing happened. It had died. He heard the shuffling again. It seemed to come from the bottom of the steps. This time someone was walking up the steps. Immediately he rushed back. His heart was racing like mad, his breathing was very fast, and his hands tingling. Just before he reached the top of the staircase, he

stumbled, banging his head against the doorstep, slumping across the steps.
A woman ascended from the coal cellar and sat next to Wayne, who was lying unconsciousness at the top of the stairs.
'Wake up! My name is Kathleen. My daughter Anne is looking for something. It's somewhere hidden in this flat. You must find it before it's too late. The lodger is on his way. Please wake up, and hurry. He will be here any minute. His spirit will not rest until you find it.'
Wayne woke up slowly, his head hurting terribly. Still a little bit dizzy, he crawled up the remaining steps and managed to get back into the house.
He hardly understood where he was or what he was meant to be doing. As though all memory of Kay had been wiped from his mind, he thought a voice had ordered him to find his way back into the house. He stumbled back to the door under the hanging ivy and pushed it open. But from the moment he entered the corridor, he noticed everything had changed. Someone had placed a straw hat and light blue coat on the coat stand, and there were muddy shoe prints on the floor tiles, leading towards the kitchen. A sudden cracking noise made him jump. Instead of becoming anxious, he became curious and he found himself acting on a dreamlike urge to find out what had caused the sound.

He walked further along the corridor and saw a pretty, small cupboard with a vase of sunflowers placed on it. Its doors were wide open. He knelt down, peered inside, and saw tubs of paint, brushes and a tobacco pipe sticking out of a leather pouch. At the far end of the corridor stood an easel with a paint-stained white cloth partly draped over a canvas. On a beechwood rush seat, lay an artist's palette with wet yellow, green and brown paint. Carefully, he lifted up the cloth and looked at the painting: it was an unfinished portrait of a woman wearing a scarf He wondered whether the painter was still in the flat. Dead set on finding the painter, he opened a door and faced the most lavish room he'd ever seen. It was beautifully decorated and upholstered, large sofas and old paintings lining the walls as if it were a Parisian salon, furnished with ashtrays, candelabras and lamps embossed in bronze.

Wayne felt a bit dazed and sat down on one of the plush sofas, watching the transparent white moon against a blue sky through the branches of the almond tree. He tilted his head forward, facing the floor, and spotted something odd. One of the floorboards was sticking up. He raised himself out of the sofa and lifted it up. An old metal box, covered in dust, became visible. It felt like he had found a

long-hidden treasure trove buried underneath the floor. Wayne blew away the dust, opened the lid and inside found a pencil sketch of a three-storey terraced Georgian house. The artist had lettered the wall 'Hackford Road' and the gate 'Maison Loyer'.
A familiar smell entered the lounge, and Wayne recognised it instantly. It was sweet pipe tobacco coming from the corridor. When he used to visit his grandparents on a Sunday morning, the first person he would see when he opened the door of the lounge was his grandfather, seated in an arm chair, smoking a pipe, a copper flip-ashtray standing next to him.
Wayne took the sketch and the box, walked into the corridor where he encountered an ethereal man with a pale face and a scruffy ginger beard. He was wearing an artist's smock and had a pipe clamped in a corner of his mouth. Wayne's body stiffened, staring at the man's crystal blue eyes and the white wound dressing which covered his right ear. The man looked ill, but at the same time he appeared to be calm and contented. Wayne, strangely, was not afraid.
"Do you need any help?"
The man didn't answer. He just stood there, staring at the box and the sketch in Wayne's hands.
"I just found this underneath the floor. Were you

looking for this?"
Somewhere in the back of his mind, Wayne felt surprised at himself for feeling so calm - but it seemed that he knew what to do without knowing how he knew.
The painter pointed at the words written on the sketch and stretched out his arms. Wayne handed him the pencil sketch. At the moment when they were both holding on to the sketch, Wayne felt a warm spiritual energy surrounding them. Reading his mind, he knew the man had a story to tell.
"You pointed at the words 'Hackford Road', please tell me, what happened?"
'I came here today to find this sketch and my mission is to return it to the Loyer family. A long time ago I lodged in an attic room at 87 Hackford Road in Brixton in a Georgian terraced house opposite the Durand School. It was owned by Ursula Loyer. I sketched the building with pencil and named it 'Maison Loyer', and hid it under the floor underneath my bed.
'I fell in love with my landlady's daughter, Eugénie Loyer, but unfortunately, she did not return my love. I was completely absorbed and mesmerised by her beauty. Instead of me, she married another man, and that sparked my descent into mental illness, shattering all my dreams. My love life was nothing short of disastrous, I was used to it. Always attracted to women in trouble,

thinking I could help them.

'Many years later, after I had become a driven but penniless painter, my spirit was broken, crushed, and I couldn't bear the burden on my heart any longer. After I spoke the words 'My sadness will last forever', my spirit finally released itself from my body in the small room at an auberge in the village of Auvers in northern France where I had spent the last days of my life.

Eugénie's grand daughter Kathleen Maynard, who was moving house to Brighton, was clearing out the house in Devon when she came across a dusty and tea-stained sketch kept in a metal box with some old photographs in the attic. Kathleen remembered that her father once said the sketch had been drawn by one of her grand mother's lodgers. She took it with her to her new flat in Brighton, and kept it underneath the floorboards until she passed away. Her flat was auctioned off, but all her belongings remained in the flat, untouched as the developer was in the process of purchasing the house. The flat has been unoccupied ever since Kathleen's death until someone moved in earlier this year.

Kathleen's daughter Anne had been looking for the sketch for so many years, but she was unable to find it. As a last resort, she went to her great-grandfather's grave and she begged him to return the sketch to the Loyer family, where it belongs. At the same time, I was paying homage to Eugénie who was buried next to her father,

and I overheard her saying every single word.
Today I came here to find the sketch and, thanks to you, I can return it to Eugénie's great-grand-daughter Anne. Now my mission has finally been completed, I'm no longer filled with sadness, and I hope my spirit can finally rest in peace.'

It was early evening and the man had a train to catch to Devon. He put on his light blue coat, placed the straw hat on his head and walked up the steps. Wayne stared through the window, following his movements. The man with the distant crystal-blue eyes looked back, tipped his hat, and a smile appeared on his face. Wayne watched him go through the large branches of the almond blossom, and hoped it would be a clear starry night.

Wayne decided to leave and walked into the corridor when the canvas caught his eye. It looked different, and then he realised the painting of the woman he had seen earlier had disappeared. Instead, there was a painting of a simple rush chair sat empty, a pipe placed on it, symbolic of its absent owner. A feeling of loneliness and devastation was present in this picture. Silently he closed the door behind him and walked up the narrow steps.

Kay waited outside Waitrose with a bag of food, drinks and a bunch of sunflowers, but there was no sign of Wayne. She called his mobile which went straight to voicemail. She was worried and walked back to the flat, where, at the bottom of the steps, she found Wayne lying down in front of the open door. She dropped her shopping, knelt down next to him and put her ear close to his face. "Thank goodness. You're breathing!" She took his wrist and checked his pulse. "Wayne, are you ok? Please, wake up!"

He opened his eyes. "Kay? What ... what am I doing here ... what happened?"

"Glad to hear you talking. I don't know what happened, but I think you have been unconscious. You were adamant you wanted to go into the flat and the last thing you said was that there was 'something about this place'. I said it was wrong and went off to the supermarket, only to find you here slumped on the floor with a bump on your head."

Wayne slowly touched his head and felt the bump. "It still hurts. I can't remember a single thing of what happened, I guess I must have tripped over something. I'm feeling much better now you're here, seeing your lovely face. I love the bunch of sunflowers you brought with you."

"I was worried when I found you, but I'm glad to hear you're feeling better. A gentleman with a straw hat and a ginger beard gave the flowers to me. I'm

sure it was the same man I saw across the road earlier, he said he's an artist and sells his canvasses in the small art gallery opposite."
Wayne's memory came back and he recalled meeting a man in the flat, fitting the same description. "Would you believe me if I told you I found a metal box with a sketch of Hackford Road, hidden under the floorboards in the basement flat, and gave it to the same man?"
"What on earth are you on about?" exclaimed Kay. "Looking under the floorboards in somebody else's house? Sounds like you've decided to become a part-time burglar!"
"No, no," said Wayne, rubbing his head slowly and beginning to get up off the floor. "It wasn't like that … I can't quite get it right in my mind. You'll just have to believe me. I'll tell you more when I can make sense of it all. *Can* I make sense of it?"
"I guess only you know the answer to that. Anyway, let's call it a night, I need to be back at the primary school tomorrow."
"The primary school? I thought you worked in an academy?"
She laughed: "Well, your memory seems to be perfectly alright. I completely forgot to tell you but our school is changing names after a last minute meeting last week. The Durand Academy will be

renamed the Van Gogh Primary. Apparently the Dutch painter used to live in the same road." Kay looked at her watch.
"Oh gosh, it's getting late. Why don't we walk back to Western Road where we can hop on a bus and get back to the cottage?"
"Yes, let's do that, I'm knackered and could do with a little snooze."
"That's a good idea, and whilst you're having a rest, I'll be packing our bags so we can leave early in the morning."

The following year, as part of a major exhibition, the London house in Hackford Road opened its doors to the public. It was the house where the famous painter lived during his twenties. Kay and Wayne attended one of the tours during the opening week. The owners had preserved the stairs, the floorboards and a pristine mantelpiece in Van Gogh's room dating from the painter's time. The house was originally owned by a mother and her daughter, Ursula and Eugénie, who ran a small school in the front room and supplemented their income with lodgers. On the walls of the small room, where the painter used to work and sleep, were several paintings and letters by the artist. In the corner of the room, displayed on an easel, stood a painting with hints of brown, green, and yellow, showing strong contrasts between light and dark, resembling a woman wearing a scarf. The painter only used a few colours: ochre for the hands and face, and green for the background and clothing. The woman with the scarf was Eugénie, and displayed the admirer's deep and strong romantic affection for her. Kay gasped. Looking at the painting was like looking at herself in a mirror, the resemblance was so strong. Wayne stared from the portrait to Kay and back again, feeling vaguely that he had seen this painting before somewhere.

"It could be a picture of you, Kay!" he whispered, as he bent forward to read the information about the painting.

In the description next to the portrait, Wayne read it was painted during one of Vincent's visits to Brighton back in 1873/1874. It ended with the painter's words, found on a letter in this very same room.

'Living with someone you love, can be lonelier than living entirely alone, if the one you love doesn't love you.
In France I turned to painting, my requited love, reminding me that life goes on, and that our sorrow and our creative vitality spring from the same heart.'

Deryk

During my life as a brewer, spare time was precious. But as I brewed most of my beer during the winter, I had the privilege of travelling to other towns and cities during the summer, stocking up my ales at inns and visiting old friends, some of them living in London, the biggest city in the kingdom with a population of about 200,000. Most towns and villages were small and people made their living from farming and fishing. Many people built sturdy 'half-timbered' houses, made with a timber frame filled in with wattle and wickerwork and plaster. Roofs were usually thatched, though some well-off people had tiles. Wealthy people covered their floors with rushes or reeds, which they strewed with sweet-smelling herbs, and lit their homes with beeswax candles.
Several years after I opened the brewery and inn, things started to change. As a result of rapidly growing industry and trade overseas, towns grew larger. The mining of coal, tin and lead flourished, as did the iron industry. During this period, England became rich and upper class and middle class people benefited from the growing wealth of the country. However, for the poor life did not improve. For them, life was hard and jobs were not easy to find.

The people in Brighthelmstone were a friendly community, and they offered a helping hand to anyone who needed it, hence it attracted a lot of beggars. The old and poor and less abled people were given licences to beg, and some of them even pretended to be mentally ill or disabled in order to beg. Some were given shelter by the local fishermen in their wooden net-shops and rope houses on the beach below the cliff, and in return the beggars would help them out by making nets for hunting and fishing and rotating the capstans to haul up boats, singing songs as they walked around the capstan.
However, anyone roaming without a licence to beg was tied to a cart in the nearest market town and whipped. Punishment in the sixteenth century was harsh and it was public. The more gruesome the punishment, the more people would attend. Minor crimes such as blasphemy, arson and prostitution were punished by the pillory or the stocks to humiliate people, but more serious crimes such as treason, heresy and murder were punished by death. Most common people were burned, hanged, or crushed between iron plates, though beheading was reserved for the wealthy. The offender's biggest fear was to be imprisoned. People were often held in prison for months before their trial, when the prisoner was given the verdict.
Brighthelmstone was a busy little fishing town occupied and visited by craftsmen, fish traders, iron mongers,

spiritual leaders, smugglers, alchemists, writers, sailors and brothel owners. The streets were narrow, sometimes cobblestoned, but mainly unpaved. The town consisted of four streets simply called North, West, South and East Street. Farmers lived here as well as the fishermen, and the fishermen called the area between East Street and Middle Street 'Hempshere'. The narrow streets functioned as pathways built between the allotments, where they grew hemp to use the bast fibre for their nets, ropes and sailcloths, and during the summer the air was filled with the intense and distinctive smell of hemp.
The fishermen lived in houses on the beach, called the 'Lower Town', within close reach of their boats and there were over eighty vessels moored on the beach. Often I went to visit the fish market at the bottom of Great East Street opposite the cliffs, to buy freshly-caught cod.
The farmers lived in a village above the cliffs so their cattle could graze in the green grassland. On Saturdays they sold pheasants, beef, veal and geese at the market.
Nothing could beat the smell of bacon coming from the general market where goods of all kinds were sold like eggs, flour, herbs, leather, spices and wood. In the eyes of many, the town was full of heretics and sorcerers, but until now nobody seemed to bother too much about what was going on down here.
The town was an eclectic mix of local people, from London, and overseas, and gossip was quickly spread by

word of mouth. People who visited the inn told me that times in the city were changing, and sooner or later our town would feel the sting of the Church.
The boy king, Edward, only nine years old when he ascended the throne and Henry VIII's only male heir, was leading a troublesome life. The king was getting weaker day after day. Neighbouring countries were aware and the English armies suffered reverses of fortune in France and Scotland. In Cornwall the Roman Catholics rose up in the 'Prayer Book Rising' caused by the changes which were introduced by the government of the new king, including the extension of the Reformation in England and Wales. Religious processions and pilgrimages were banned, and commissioners were sent out to remove all symbols of Catholicism. Given Edward's poor constitution it was clear he would not survive long. It became more and more apparent that this would open the door to his sister Mary to ascend the throne, and it would have a major impact on many people living in this country, including me.

Booking Six

Jim and Joe lived in a fashionable and lavish flat in Soho. Jim had worked as a bar-tender in the Royal Vauxhall Tavern, where many years ago Freddie Mercury, allegedly smuggled in Princess Diana disguised as a man. He made a career-move and became one of the most popular d.j's in the 'nearby nightclub The Eagle', playing massive disco tunes from back in the day. Joe was into underground music and landed a job at Sedition, tucked away under a supermarket near Old Street, attracting beardy hipsters, edgy drag queens and trendy girls. They called Brighton their second home and after a night of clubbing on the coast they usually crashed out at their oldest friends' Donna and Abi's. They received an invitation from Donna and Abi to attend their wedding. For this special occasion, they splashed out for a booking at the Black Lion Cottage, just around the corner from the Town Hall where their mates would get married.

Jim returned to the cottage from a shopping-spree in the Lanes, carrying several glossy bags containing brand-new designer shirts, trousers, briefs and socks. He bought two fabulous shirts for himself and Joe to wear at their friends' wedding, and a black-coloured shirt with golden crowns he would wear during his next shift at The Eagle, a shirt fit for a king, or even a queen. He loved boutique-shopping though it cost him an arm and a leg. He felt like he had run half a marathon. Fancying a quick shot of caffeine, he was making himself a fresh cup of espresso when he heard someone opening the front door. It was Joe who had just returned from his own shopping-spree.

"Hi darling. I'm making myself an espresso. Do you fancy one?"

"Yes please, that would be nice!" Joe picked up his designer bags and walked into the room.

"Well, well, well!" Jim said, greatly surprised about the amount of bags Joe had brought in. "Just a little bit of shopping then? How much did you spend?" he said sarcastically, trying to sneak a peek into the bags.

"Don't ask, and get your nose out of there. They've got some fantastic shops down here. I literally had to drag myself out!"

"Talking of drag, I just met a woman called Laura dressed in period costume outside the tourist office representing the Regency Town House in Hove. The house is being restored to its original state by a team

of volunteers headed by curator Nick Tyson. She seemed very keen to promote this place and gave me these brochures about the house. Have a look. It's a nineteenth century living museum and they're having an open day today. She also told me it's haunted. Fancy going there?"
Jim flicked through the brochure containing stunning pictures of stairwells, open fire places, and stories about ghost sightings. "Allegedly several guests have said the house is haunted after they had seen the spirit of a man in the basement. Sounds like there have been quite a few unexplained deaths in the place too - murders! A great place for ghosts then! Let's go!"

From the seafront, they spotted Brunswick Square, an iconic square with beautiful terraced houses and Regency architecture facing the sea. The house was decorated with bunting in many bright colours and a life-size cutout of a man dressed in a dark blue frock coat and top hat was placed on the elegant steps leading to the front door. Jim and Joe were welcomed by ladies dressed in period costume, guiding them into the dark hallway underneath the framed colourful stained glass window, creating a striking first impression. The ladies suggested that they waited in the kitchen in the basement, should

they want to take part in the next guided tour. Jim smelled the aroma of fresh coffee coming from the kitchen downstairs.
"If you wish, you can have a coffee or tea and a home-made cake?" said the lady in a period green dress, white blouse and cap, which were slightly at variance with her modern designer spectacles. "The cakes are based on a historical recipe from a Regency cookbook made by our lovely cook, Paul. I would highly recommend them. But beware, they say the house is haunted, and visitors have reported seeing a man roaming the corridors dressed in black." The lady put her finger onto her lips, shushing them, and pointed toward the staircase leading down to the basement before she quietly walked back to the entrance door to greet new visitors.
Jim and Joe walked down the staircase into a narrow, gloomy corridor with a red brick floor, set below a dimmed amber lamp hanging from the high ceiling. When Jim walked past the restored wooden-panelled staircase, he noticed a distinct draught coming from between the joints. It was an old house with a mysterious atmosphere, a place where you rather would not be left alone, especially not at night. They walked past the butler's parlour and stopped in front of a yellow door. Would this door

open to a kitchen filled with fresh coffee and cakes?
Jim turned the door handle. "This can't be right!"
He looked puzzled. "The door's locked!" Jim was looking at Joe. "You don't happen to have a paperclip or skeleton key on you, do you?"
"Seriously, do I look like I might have a skeleton key on me? And even if I did, it would not be appropriate to pick the lock. Why don't we just go back upstairs and ask one of the ladies to assist?"
"Ok, but before we do that, let's try once more."
Jim tried the handle again, putting his ear to the door. "It's still locked, and I can't hear any noises in there. Can you hear anything?"
"This isn't one of your jokes is it?" As Joe tried the handle himself the door didn't budge so he listened. "No, I can't hear anything either. Are you sure this is the right place?"
They were both standing with their ears pressed against the door, looking at each other, puzzled, when Jim noticed a light reflecting in the high gloss paint of the door, growing brighter. When they turned to look around, they were facing a man, standing right in front of them, holding an old brass oil lamp. His top hat was pulled down, shading his eyes. The man raised the oil lamp and, as he started to turn down the flame, Jim spotted a silver signet ring on his hand glinting in the fading light. As the

flame diminished, so too did Jim and Joe, losing consciousness, and slumped to the floor, overwhelmed by the strong smell of the oil lamp. It was the same oil lamp, which had been used for nearly two hundred years by one of Miss Buckhurst's live-in servants, Stephen.

On an early morning in 1851 Stephen opened the door and inhaled the musty smell of the damp, dark kitchen and put the oil lamp on the table. He turned up the wick and its light illuminated the spacious kitchen, giving it a cosy warm glow. The floor was laid with grey and red tiles in a diamond pattern. The door of the pantry on his left was open, and he could see bottles of ale, jam and preserves, pickles and cheeses. To his right was a large red brick open fireplace over which hung an impressive mirror with a silver gilded frame. The mirrored glass reflected the light of the oil lamp onto the tall dresser displaying the finest bone china: cups and saucers, plates, and cake stands. There wasn't much time, as he had to get the kitchen ready before the guests arrived. He thoroughly polished the fireplace, placed a few wooden logs in the hearth and carefully took the required cutlery and crockery from the dresser. During the early nineteenth century it was not unusual for servants to get up at five a.m. on a dark winter morning to start cleaning out ashes and polishing hearths, before lighting the new day's fires. Within half an hour the kitchen was filled with the hot air displacing the ever present damp smell, and Stephen left to light the oil lamps in the other rooms.

Later that day, Lady Buckhurst's lady's maid, Miss Prosser, entered the kitchen. "Laura? Is Cook here?"
"No ma'am. Can I help?" She was sitting on a chair with a pan full of peeled potatoes and had put the knife down on the wooden table. Outside, rain was lashing against the sash-windows, leaving the small courtyard outside completely flooded. Inside, it was nice and warm, the kitchen was filled with heavenly smells of roasting meat.
"What's for dinner tonight?" Miss Prosser enquired.
"Partridge wrapped in sliced pork and apple-sauce," Laura answered with a respectful smile.
"That sounds delicious. On another note, the oil lamps upstairs need to be refilled. You haven't seen Stephen, have you Laura?"
"I'm afraid I haven't seen him. If we've run out of lamp oil perhaps Stephen has noticed it, and he might have gone into town to get some," Laura suggested.
"In this weather? It's raining cats and dogs," she

snapped at her.
"Perhaps Stephen has taken an umbrella with him."
Miss Prosser gave her a sharp look. "When was the last time you saw him, Laura?"
"I saw him around noon when we had lunch. I can go to the shop and have a look for him now, if you like?'
"Yes, I *would* like that," she said and ushered Laura out of the kitchen.
Miss Prosser boiled some water for tea and walked to the dresser to get a cup and saucer. She frowned when she noticed a single plate on the drainer. Didn't Laura just say she had lunch with Stephen around noon? Why was there only a single plate on the draining rack? This didn't ring true. Miss Prosser left the kitchen and walked upstairs to see if she could find Stephen.
Earlier that day Stephen had noticed that the lamp oil was low and had indeed gone to the merchant to get some, returning late morning. He entered the kitchen and put the oil in the store room. At the same moment, he heard a loud banging noise coming from the paved area outside the kitchen window. The wind was rattling through the single-pane sash windows, an earthy smell was entering the kitchen. Through the swaying curtains he saw somebody outside, it was Laura, knocking loudly on

the window. Relieved it was she, he lifted up the window.
"You gave me a fright," he said.
"Sorry about the noise, Stephen, I dropped the potato sack, it was too heavy. I left my knife on the kitchen table, and I need it to open it. Would you mind?" asked Laura.
He picked up the knife and gently handed it to her.
"Thank you, Stephen. I'm sorry, but ... "
"What's up, Laura?" Stephen looked at Laura waiting for an explanation.
"I'm sorry if I've been acting strange lately."
"Do you mean for ignoring and avoiding me? I just don't understand why you've been behaving this way. Is it something I've said? Something I've done wrong?"
"I always did everything you asked me to do: 'Yes, sir, anything's else sir?"
"I'm sorry but I have no other way off putting this; that's what you're hired for."
"But I also made your bed, brought you breakfast and ironed your clothes?"
"That's true, you did but I thought you were trying to be nice?"
"I was trying to be nice to you and, this is the first time I'm saying it out loud. I have strong romantic feelings towards you, but, you never

returned it."
"Laura, I ... I had no idea. I'm not very good in picking up any signals, probably because I'm not looking for a relationship - I'm married!"
"I know you are and I appreciate you're not looking for anyone else but I've been in so much pain, I've been grieving. This is all your fault!"
"My fault?"
"You could have had me, but, I'm afraid it's too late now."
Laura raised the knife above her head and with great force the knife cut deeply into Stephen's chest. His body fell on the floor, releasing an eerie translucent figure, disappearing from his body through the swaying curtains. The house had a secret, and Laura vowed it would never, ever be revealed.

When Jack, a volunteer of the house had finished the guided tour, he walked down to the corridor to make himself a cup of tea. Just before he reached the kitchen he was startled to see Jim and Joe slumped against the wall, both looking a little dazed.
"Are you both okay?" he asked.
"I think so." Joe rubbed his temples, coming around. "We found ourselves leaning against the wall, and to be honest, we can't remember what happened."

Jack helped them to stand up. "I think you could do with a cup of hot sweet tea for the shock?"
"That would be lovely."
Jack easily turned the handle of the door they had failed to open and they followed him into the kitchen. They could not understand how they had been unable to open the door earlier.
The kitchen was at the heart of the house, and for the occasion was turned into a lovely tea room with round tables laid with white lace tablecloths and little crystal vases with violet, pink and white flowers. In past times, most affluent Victorian upper-class households had servants, and most kitchens were designed and built as a contained space, used exclusively for cooking, that could be closed. Instead, this room was now used as a meeting place where guests could talk, eat, and drink watching coffee, tea and cakes being made in a semi-open pantry. From the moment they had walked in, they inhaled the smells of oven-baked cakes and pastries mixed with the bergamot and lemon of Earl Grey tea. Jim picked up the china cup and saucer, beautifully decorated with pink and violet roses, and after a couple of sips he started to feel much better. A lady dressed in period costume walked in and brought them a slice of lemon-drizzle cake.
"Sir, would you like a knife for the cake?" asked the

lady.
"Yes, please." As Joe took the knife, he realised her voice sounded familiar. "Oh Laura, it's you! I didn't recognise you at first!" Laura was dressed in a black period dress, and a white blouse accompanied by a beautiful velvet hat.
"Jim, this is Laura. I told you about her this morning."
"Yes, I do remember. Laura, you look beautiful, like the belle of the ball. Period clothes really suit you."
"Thank you for the compliment, Jim. I hope you'll enjoy the cake. It's from a nineteenth century cookbook."
"How wonderful, an authentic recipe! That's so classy."
After he had eaten the sumptuous cake, Jim looked at his watch. "It's five to one, the guided tour is about to start."
"Actually if you don't mind, I'll give the tour a miss as I fancy another piece of cake." said Joe." You'd better hurry."

As Jim walked up the staircase, the front door was flung open. A bitter cold wind entered the long gloomy hallway accompanied by cold rain, lashing onto the floor. Instinctively Jim ran to the door and closed it. When he turned around, a man was

standing close behind him. He took a step back and recognised him. It was the same man he had encountered earlier in the basement, carrying a brass oil lamp with a flickering flame.
"Who are you? Why are you following me?" Jim said keeping his distance as the scent of oil was making him feel dizzy again.
At the same moment, the storm eased down and from the end of the corridor, he heard the sound of shoes clicking on the floor, entering the hallway. Slightly dizzy, he could hear the voices of Joe and Laura calling his name, rushing towards him.
"Are you alright? We heard the front door bang and wondered what had happened." Joe gave him a hug.
"I'm alright. The same man was here, the one we met downstairs and he disappeared just before you arrived. He must be in the house, somewhere."
"I just knew something wasn't right. It's weird you've seen the man again."
Jim let go of Joe, and his eyes widened as he spotted a painting on the wall behind him. "Now that's creepy," he murmured, peering at it, "Look, that guy in the painting, he is the spitting image of the man with the oil lamp."
Joe turned around, looked at the painting and nodded. "Yes, it's definitely him."
Jim took a closer look at the painting. It depicted a

wealthy aristocratic-looking woman and a group of her household servants in the background. There was the man they had seen with the oil lamp - a tall serious figure in black; and next to him was a woman standing on the left in the painting, dressed in a black period dress, white blouse set off by a beautiful velvet hat. He was holding his breath when he read the year it was painted, it was 1849. Jim turned his face to Laura.

"Wow, you've really copied this exact portrait, haven't you? In incredible detail too!"

Jim turned his gaze to the picture again, noticing that not only had every element of the clothing been reproduced in Laura's costume, down to the last button, but that the face - the face of the woman in the portrait - was exactly the same. He turned to look at her again, knowing as he did so that she sensed he had seen her image in the painting wearing the same costume, the face unchanged by time. She was the same person standing in front of him nearly two centuries later. This was impossible.

Swiftly, Laura pulled a kitchen knife from underneath her apron and pointed it towards the couple.

"It's a shame you found out." Laura said. "You're so young. The others were so much older."

"Which others?" Jim asked with a quivering voice.

"Several others discovered my secret: I look exactly like the lady in the painting. Yes! Of course I do!" She broke into a chilling peal of laughter and raised the knife above her head. "Do you think Time can heal my anger? Never. You're not going to leave this house alive. You have to be silenced."
Before she could cause any harm, a man jumped between them and quickly grabbed Laura's knife. It was the spirit of Stephen, the long gone missing servant of Lady Buckhurst, fatally stabbed by Laura in the kitchen. The woman shrank back against the wall, staring wild-eyed at the man she had killed so many years before. For a moment, her dreadful, murderous energy had ebbed away as suddenly as it had come.
Nervously Stephen looked at Jim and Joe. "I think I owe you an apology. It was my fault you couldn't access the kitchen after you arrived - all I wanted to do was to protect you from Laura, who was left by herself in the kitchen after all the guests had gone upstairs to join an earlier guided tour. When she is left in a room with one or two people, she wants to take control of the situation and can become unpredictably dangerous. I simply could not bear the thought of your throats being slashed by this maleficent woman, who has cruelly cut off the lives of so many innocent people seemingly without any

motive. For this is the terrible secret that at last I'm able to share: she murdered me. She put my dead body into the potato sack and dumped it in the well in the patio. Yes, she stabbed me in senseless anger - and then, not long afterwards, a freak accident took her life too. The cording of the old sash window in the kitchen was frayed - we all knew it needed replacing - and it broke one day as she was leaning out. The heavy frame hurtled down, the glass shattered and a large shard severed her neck. But not even death could stop her thirst for blood - and I have watched helplessly as she fades from helpless headless ghost and back again, always driven endlessly by the same madness. Today my spirit wanted to roam the rooms of the house when something happened, totally unexpected. When I passed the mirror on the first floor I saw myself reflected in the glass and I looked different, instead of looking straight through myself, the mirror reflected my matured body wearing clothes and even my ring. It all happened without any explanation. I knew something had given me the energy to manifest more completely on the plane of the living - perhaps it was the sheer force of my despair over so many years - and this meant that at last I would be able to tackle Laura. Her mad anger has made her able to interact with the material plane and cause untold suffering, as no other spirit has ever been able to do. At last I saw my chance! So when you discovered Laura hadn't aged, and she pulled out the knife, I came to your rescue, just in time. And now I have the strength to finish this job, this terrible memory which has played out again and again. Slowly he turned to Laura. "Your mad and violent behaviour has to stop. This was your last attempt to kill innocent people and I'm sure our guests would agree that your presence is no longer required in this house. My promise to you is, that I will oblige to their wish. This is goodbye, forever." He lifted the knife, and in one swift movement Laura's head was severed from her body, her clothes crumpled to the floor, and that was all that was left of her. Nobody was able to explain what happened to her body or her severed head.

The following day, after a sudden downpour, Lisa, an author and medium communicating with the living and the deceased, arrived at the Regency Town House to attend a ghost writing workshop. Her coat was soaking wet. From the moment she entered the house, she sensed a dramatic atmosphere, and put the dripping umbrella in the stand in the porch. She instinctively felt something was wrong in this house, sensing that something terrible had happened here: and her feelings proved her right. Her powerful presence had not gone unnoticed. A woman, dressed in a Victorian dress stained in blood and wearing a large white bonnet cap, emerged from the immense wall painting, and stepped into the hallway. Instead of panicking, Lisa as an experienced medium, acted as if it was something not out of the ordinary to her and acted as though that the woman was welcoming her to the house.

"Excuse me, could you tell me whether this is the right place for the work shop?"

The woman ignored her and walked through the the hallway, disorientated, her hands touching the wall trying to find her way to the front of the house. Lisa was perplexed as she had felt the change in atmosphere. "Are you ok?"

Instead of a confrontation, the woman walked past her without noticing her, and when she reached the front door, her white cap dropped onto the floor. Lisa looked at her and to her dismay, she saw why she had not made any eye contact and why she didn't say a word. A white cap lay on the floor, revealing the woman's headless body. The story was true. The ghost of a beheaded woman, dressed in Victorian clothes covered in stained blood, still haunted the house.

At the very same moment, the door flung itself open. Laura knew her time had come. She floated through the doorway, gently rising into a dark grey sky above the house whilst the rain was streaming down the tall bay windows, falling into the basement, releasing her from her fear, her pain, and her vengeful feelings. Whilst the sky cried, everything faded away into the sky, and for the first time she was surrounded by light reaching for the endless sky. The nature the house had so desperately craved, entered a little at a time. Vases with fresh flowers appeared in the hallway, sumptuous apple pies were cooked in the kitchen, and warm glows of sunshine brightened up the rooms. Stephen watched Laura's spirit go, and gently closed the door behind her, for good.

Deryk

Occasionally, I passed through the small village of Hove, built at the foot of the open chalk hills. The land was rural with long fields set at right angles to the beach, stretching out north to Blatchington, Hangleton and Preston. There was an old church, St Andrew's, standing quite a good distance from the shore, midway between the old churches of Aldrington and Brighthelmstone, and all three were joined by one road, called Church Road by the few locals who lived there. Goldstone, situated north of the church site, was believed to be built on the site of a mystical stone circle, as the ancients picked up the fact that the valley had lines of influence emanating from underground streams. The original village was situated along Hove Street, consisting of a Manor House with stables and a few fishermen's flint stone cottages built along the street and the foreshore. There was also an old barn and stables with a flint wall on the south side, while the level stretches of Aldrington were still virtually undeveloped. The Ship Inn was built at the seaward end, attracting many fishermen and rogue smugglers selling their produce. The inn carried a coat of arms which included a ship at the top of the crest commemorating the French attacks on the coast of Hove.

One evening I visited The Ship Inn, a character-filled place where I was welcomed by the innkeeper whilst his staff stabled my horse in the livery yard at the back of the house. In the back room I met Father George Ashburner, who had had a little bit too much to drink, and he revealed that the sacred edifice of St Andrew's was so deserted that local smugglers used it as a place to store their contraband such as brandy. I thanked him for confiding in me. Sitting next to the log fire, the innkeeper came over to me and offered me a drink, briefing me about the latest news about King Edward VI. Landowners, travelling down from London with the intention to enclose land and convert it to sheep pasturage, had told him the latest news. Apparently, when Edward VI became mortally ill, he planned to exclude Mary from the line of succession as she would reverse the Protestant reforms he had promoted during his reign. His advisers, however, told him that he could not disinherit only one of his half-sisters, he would have to disinherit his other sister Elizabeth as well. Edward felt forced to exclude both from the line of succession in his will.

On his death, leading politicians proclaimed Lady Jane Grey as Queen, but Mary assembled a force in East Anglia and deposed Jane who was subsequently beheaded. Mary ascended the throne and became Queen Mary I, Queen of England. Her sister, Princess Elizabeth, was imprisoned in the Tower of London and then placed under house arrest at Woodstock. Mary married Philip of Spain, and became known for her aggressive attempt to reverse the English Reformation. Revalidation of heresy legislation including the 'De haeritico comburendo' (Concerning the burning of the heretics), led the way to prosecutions of Protestants. Soon visitors told me the horrific news that Protestants were sent to Newgate Prison where they would be kept, awaiting a long trial before they would be burned at the stake all over the country to mark the restoration of Roman Catholicism in England and Ireland. 'Bloody' Mary's dark mission had began.

Beyond Newgate Prison, was an asylum called Bethlem, the place where people with mental health issues were kept. They were called lunatics as it was believed then that the moon affected their minds, much as the moon affected the tides. Some of the prisoners had been captured in battles and incarcerated there. Before King Edward VI ascended the throne, the Lord Mayor of London, Sir John Gresham, petitioned the Crown to grant Bethlem to the city. However, Henry VIII was reluctant to cede the custody, order and governance of the hospital. One year later the Mayor of the City of London purchased the hospital and its possessions from the King and by Royal Letters Patent re-established it as a hospital for lunatics.

Booking Seven

Henry, a well-established fashion designer and tailor creating the most extravagant costumes for celebrities, occupied a Georgian townhouse. His house overlooked Grosvenor Square, a beautiful and much loved Green in central London, with wonderfully maintained lawns, statues, and memorials. The development of modern fashion had its roots in nineteenth century design, renowned for its gowns, riding dress, bonnets and top hats, the period in which fashionable clothing became widely available to wealthy English society. Fascinated by Georgian fashion, Henry started creating his own Georgian-inspired costumes, eventually replacing his entire wardrobe with perfectly-tailored handmade knee-high leather riding boots, shirts with ruffled lace jabots and cuffs and stylish riding jackets with long tails. When he was in his twenties he would wear his dandy attire outside with great pride whilst sitting on a bench in the square, or going for an occasional stroll in Hyde Park. By the time he was thirty, he became more obsessed: he would appear in public wearing his perfectly tailored dandy gear on a daily basis. Henry imagined he lived in a past society, a place which made him feel content, the nineteenth century in Britain, idealising an image of himself that increasingly bore little relation to reality. He always believed in success, and he knew the secret of how to achieve it: believe in yourself. The locals considered him to be a novelty. People took selfies with him, he became a well-known eccentric man featuring on the front pages of many newspapers, the tabloids, had interviews on television and won the most prestigious designer awards for his creations. Henry, now rich and famous, attracted the richest people of London like honeybees, he was living the life.

One day an Italian designer, Gaia Ventura, moved into Mayfair, attracting a lot of attention because of her simplistic designs which used the most vibrant colours. All eyes were focussed on her instead of Henry, whose fame was now in decline, his business suffering badly. What was her secret? Was it the book all people were talking about, *The Law of Attraction*, which allegedly held the key to success? The fact was that Henry's customers, drawn by the latest fashion and charming appearance of Gaia Ventura, placed fewer and fewer orders with him. Despite his effort to advertise his special skills online, Henry attracted only a few new customers who paid him for his outstanding services, but it wasn't enough to cover all of his bills. Within months of Gaia's arrival, there was no more work lined up, and tragically his fashion company folded. Such is the fickle trade of fashion. At that time when he frequented the square, dressed in his dandy attire, every conversation he started was about King George IV, every situation and scenario was about the Georgian period. Clinging on to this era, he dreaded to believe that anything in the present or future could possibly be better than Georgian times: a time of impeccable manners, unswerving loyalty, and elegant dress.

Henry was stuck in the past. He became a recluse, just like King George IV, isolating himself from the rest of the world in the private rooms of his Georgian townhouse. The locals no longer saw Henry sitting in the square, or going out for a walk in the park.

He thought a lot about the past, and after he stopped watching television and listening to the radio, he created his own little world, and lived in it. People who passed his house looked through the elongated rectangular windows of his lounge, and could glimpse him reading books on the chaise longue, or writing letters at his desk. The man, who once enjoyed visiting theatres like London's Drury Lane, Covent Green and the Haymarket to watch plays and musicals with his friends, eventually became too afraid to leave the house. Henry handed his letters to the postman who would kindly post them at the depot and the lovely lady who worked in the local supermarket around the corner, delivered his weekly food shop. His doctor visited him on a monthly basis to examine and prescribe him medication, as he was too anxious to visit the practice. Whatever his doctor tried, none of the remedies cured his state of mind. After Henry's doctor had exhausted all medication, he approached a consultant in the hospital, explaining his patient's situation. The consultant visited Henry at his house, where, after a two hour assessment, he was diagnosed with a personality disorder, and he became a patient in Bethlem Royal Hospital, one of the oldest psychiatric hospitals in London dating back to 1247.

Henry had already spent several months in the hospital, showing no improvement, when his psychiatrist Dr Busby came up with a radical new approach for his treatment. The doctor was skilled in the use of Clinical Hypnosis and in the course of a team meeting, he suggested that a state of deep hypnosis might enable Henry to accept suggestions that the 'past life' he believed in was over and done and that this would offer a pathway back to normal reality. The doctor would not attempt to dislodge Henry's long-held delusion (which would just lead to resistance) but planned to bring him gently to a resolution to enable him to leave the past and accept modern life. The session was arranged and Dr Busby was able to induct Henry into a deep trance and began taking him back to a life as King George IV. George was famous for his dissolute lifestyle and his palace the Royal Pavilion in Brighton. Henry imagined he lived in a past society, the nineteenth century, and he idealised an image of himself that increasingly bore little relation to reality. He was obsessed with his so-called past life, and he truly believed he was the reincarnation of the king.

The session was productive enough for further hypnosis to be indicated in Henry's treatment plan, but Dr Busby assessed that much further work would be needed before a resolution could be achieved; and meanwhile Henry believed even more strongly in his delusion.

During his second regression hypnosis session, he entered an even deeper trance, and Dr Busby asked him questions to help him express the beliefs at the root of his delusion, which he hoped to evoke

from deep inside his subconscious.
"Henry, that belief of yours about memories from a past life has been giving you some trouble lately ... and we can do something about that... so as you drift deeper and deeper into an even more comfortable state, fragments of imagery are emerging... that's it, deeper and deeper ... and some of that imagery contains information that is going to help you to feel so much better soon …"
As Dr Busby's calm voice lulled Henry into restful relaxation, his tranquil face made it clear that he was coping well with the induction, and Busby ventured further. "You can tell me anything you like now, Henry, and in a moment you're going to find it so easy and natural to talk to me about those memories as those images float up…"
Henry's slack jaw and relaxed mouth made his voice sound very different as he began to speak. "I'm in my bedchamber."
"Good, Henry," said the doctor, checking that the dictaphone was recording properly; "and what's in your bedchamber now? What's letting you know that you're ready to change and soon be more relaxed about the present time?"
Henry placed one of his pale hands on his stomach, and with the other clasped the psychiatrist's hand, and the expression on his face showed he was in

excruciating pain. "I'm dying, I'm dying, there's a violent pain in my stomach!"
Alarmed, the psychiatrist quickly wound down the session, bringing Henry back from his trance, for the experience of pain under hypnosis could be as distressing as pain in conscious reality.
"This is unbelievable," Busby said later to a colleague, as he discussed the results of the session. "George's autopsy conducted by his physicians revealed the king indeed had died from a bleeding resulting from the rupture of a blood vessel in his stomach. For many years, I have been collecting stories from my patients who claim that they can recall their past lives, but to memorise the cause of death of your past life whilst being unconscious, will call into question the idea that our humanity ends with our death."
Dr Busby's colleague shook his head. "Well, you know that there could be more than one explanation for this so-called memory. A few sentences from a book, maybe read in a history lesson years ago, can form the basis of elaborate delusions in our patients. Henry could simply have seen a television programme and retained a few simple facts. You'd need a lot more evidence than this to persuade me to question the idea that humanity ends with death, as you put it. The evidence tends rather to the

contrary!"
Dr Busby chose not to argue with his colleague, but he continued to think deeply about the case. Subsequent hypnotic inductions produced more and more detailed and accurate information. Eventually, completely baffled by the results, Dr Busby consulted his senior colleague Dr Tucker, who was an expert in regression hypnosis treatment, which aimed to gain insight into a patient's beliefs about their past to find coping methods to help them address their current problems. During his career, Dr Tucker had treated hundreds of patients, and his treatments had always been successful. One of his patients, Julia, had believed she was the reincarnation of Lady Jane Grey, the Queen who ruled for nine days, becoming an iconic figure after her execution at the hands of Mary Tudor. One day, he took Julia to the Tower of London where Jane was beheaded, followed by a trip to the National Gallery to view a painting by Paul Delaroche showing Jane blindfolded kneeling down in a white satin dress in front of a wooden block with a cast iron ring. His patient burst into tears when she saw the painting and said, sobbing, this is how she came to her end in the sixteenth century. Dr Tucker explained to her this painting was created nearly three hundred years after Jane was executed, there

were aspects of the painting which were inaccurate. In fact the execution was not conducted right in front of the chapel: instead Lady Jane was executed in the open air in a field called Tower Green. Julia's journey to the Tower and the museum had been a radical approach to therapy whereby Dr Tucker had presented an opportunity to uncover lessons from 'previous lives'. The challenge of having learned that the painting by Delaroche didn't appear to be accurate made her question her assumptions about what she thought she remembered and she promised she would apply the experience to her current lifetime and situation. As she was unable to remember exactly how she died, hundreds of years ago, she decided she wanted to overcome her obsession, promising to live her life simply as Julia.
"Perhaps you should take Henry to Brighton and visit the Royal Pavilion under strict supervision?" Dr Tucker suggested. "Let's hope it will break the fantasy and cure him of his delusion. I'm more than happy to join you, if you wish?"
"I would be pleased if you could, especially because of your experience in dealing with patients who believe they're reincarnations of historical people. A good friend of mine lives in Brighton, and he happens to rent out a three bedroom house, the Black Lion Cottage, where all of us could stay. It's

closely situated to the Royal Pavilion and I hope the visit to the palace will cure him."
"That sounds like a good idea, Charles. I was reading in *The Times* that the Royal Pavilion is hosting a new display - items originally commissioned by George IV himself, so there will be a genuine personal connection. It will be useful for Henry to experience the truth, that he can have no genuine recollection of them from his imaginary memory bank. It may help jog him back to reality Could you let 'His Royal Highness' know to dress less ostentatiously for the occasion as I would prefer not to attract any attention from other visitors."
"I will try to convince him to wear plain clothing. Perhaps it will help if I tell him he will be able to discover how the previous king impressed his guests with lavish banquets, balls and concerts."
Doctor Busby emailed his friend Matt and booked the Black Lion Cottage.

The following day the two psychiatrists and Henry left the hospital and took the train from Victoria down to Brighton, arriving at the cottage by early evening. Henry thought the accommodation was characterful and quaint, but he criticised the small rooms, the narrow stairs and the open kitchen. After the men had unpacked their bags and refreshed themselves, they went out for a bite to eat at the quirky style pub 'The Mesmerist'. They climbed up the stairs to the second floor and encountered a secret doorway, giving them access to 'The Birdcage', a room covered with elegant wallpaper with a menagerie of exotic animals and a sophisticated colour scheme of black and gold. They sat down at one of the tables, ordered their food and ended the meal with a discussion about their plans for the following day.

"I suggest we visit the Royal Pavilion mid-morning, and once we've done the tour and have seen the collection, we could have some lunch in town." Dr Busby looked at Dr Tucker.

"That's fine with me, and hopefully there won't be too many people visiting, so we can have a good look at all the objects."

After they finished their meal and drained their drinks, they had a stroll along the promenade to burn off some of the calories before they returned to the cottage. Henry walked ahead, gazing out at the sea and lost in his own thoughts; the psychiatrists followed slowly behind him, keeping him in sight but discussing other professional matters. After a while, their talk took another turn.

"I'm sorry for changing the subject," Dr Tucker interrupted, "but have there ever been any reports about ghost sightings of George IV? The reason why I'm bringing this up is that I've visited the palace before, and some of the rooms felt a bit creepy to me."

"Interestingly enough, there are no historical records of anyone having seen the ghost of George IV, or even his wife or mistress," Dr Busby responded; "but some mysterious sightings, ghostly sounds have been heard throughout the maze of the estate and the secret tunnel. Several members of staff have reported the sounds of regular footsteps in the underground passageways of Brighton Dome, with the sound being so realistic that they were convinced of being joined by a colleague. One worker even shouted out: 'Go away! Leave me alone!' only to find that the tunnels were empty, but the footsteps still carried on."

"Oh, I do remember now. One of my friends used to work for the Registrar Office, and told me she once walked into the Music Room and could hear a piano playing, when the ghost of King George IV appeared in front of her, wearing a plain waistcoat, a pair of silk trousers, and black hessian riding boots. She fainted and was found by her superintendent. The experience left her terrified, and she told me she couldn't sleep for days."

Dr Busby rolled his eyes. "Well, let's hope we don't

encounter any ghosts tomorrow. After all we're here to help George, not to frighten him with ghost stories."

After this they returned to the cottage. The psychiatrists were a little bit sleepy after all the food they had eaten and could do with a nap. Dr Busby locked the front door and both men went upstairs to their bedrooms to have a snooze.

Henry decided to stay in the lounge and sat down on the sofa. He heard people walking past the front door, singing and laughing. The group probably had a little bit too much to drink. Drawn by the noise, he looked at the door, and noticed that Dr Busby had left the keys in the lock. This would be the perfect opportunity to visit the Royal Pavilion, by himself. He waited a good fifteen minutes to make sure the men were fast asleep, then grabbed his coat and the keys, and nipped out into Brighton's busy nightlife. He walked past the Italian restaurant and the Town Hall, turned left, and when he reached the end of East Street he saw the entrance gate to the Royal Pavilion. People, wearing their newest colourful outfits, walked down North Street on their way to the nightclubs. He crossed the bottom of North Street, situated next to the Old Steine, walked through the magnificent Indian-style domed gate resting on four pillars, and entered the Pavilion

Gardens. Unlike the buzz in North Street, it was very quiet, there was hardly anyone there. For a moment he took in the tranquil atmosphere of the Regency gardens, with lampposts softly shining their light on the lawns and beds of mixed shrubs and floral plants crossed by curving paths, shrubs, trees, and flowers. He followed the path, passing benches with homeless people all curled up in their sleeping bags, and turned right where the path mysteriously ended in front of a corner pavilion with four minarets at the north side of the palace.

Henry stopped at the end of the path and stared at the French windows of the king's apartments which looked across the western lawns. The sound of muffled footsteps broke the silence and he turned around. There was nobody else there, except him. The sound of echoing footsteps continued, it was nearby, and they moved towards the corner pavilion before they faded away. Instead of coming from above the ground, could it be that the sound had travelled from underground? He recalled the conversation he had overheard during their walk this evening about the 'secret tunnel' between the Brighton Dome linked to the Royal Pavilion by an underground passage, and he was sure he heard the echoing sound of someone's shoes beneath him. Below a stone verandah, supported by a row of leaf

columns, Henry saw a dimmed light behind one of the windows. This was rather unusual as the palace was closed at this time of the night, and he wondered whether someone had forgotten to switch off the lights. Inquisitively, he walked towards it, and to his surprise he saw a thin white curtain blowing through a door opening at the end of the colonnade. Someone had not only forgotten about the light, they also had forgotten to close the door.
He stepped into a hallway with high ceilings, and heard the beautiful sound of a piano in the air. It seemed to come from the adjacent rooms. Interested to find out where the heavenly sound was coming from, Henry opened the nearest door, and ended up in the King's private rooms consisting of a study, a dressing room, a bathroom and a bedroom. The walls, covered with a printed green dragon paper, had been closed to the public since the nineteenth century but there was no sign of a piano. Henry started to feel tired. He lay down on the bed and closed his eyes. Drifting away, further and further, his head filled itself with colourful dreams.

He woke up to the sound of soft voices. The voices came from the adjacent room, where probably the sound of the piano had come from before he fell asleep. Henry got up, walked towards the red-

japanned decorated door, and opened it. He saw a group of approximately twenty smartly-dressed people holding champagne flutes, chit-chatting in front of a grand piano, with light blue chinoiserie vases placed on consoles near the wall. Henry was approached by a butler holding a silver salver with champagne flutes. "Thank you for attending the 'After Hours Tour'. Could I offer you a glass of sparkling wine?" Without hesitating Henry said: "How delightful! Thank you." He took a sip, and a second butler presented a serving platter with a selection of delicious canapés. There was skewered salami and smoked ricotta cheese, crab and lime on crackers, honey and chipotle cashews and almonds. Gingerly Henry picked up one of the skewers.
"The tour will start in fifteen minutes," announced the first man to the room at large; " and there'll be plenty of time to discover the wonders of King George's dazzling seaside resort and, most of all, it's the most exotic building in Britain. This tour will allow you to see the palace in all of its evening glory, as George himself would have enjoyed it."
"Thank you for having me. I can't wait to see the palace." Henry observed the extraordinary interior of this extravagant room, and listened as the guide read aloud from a shiny pamphlet describing its

contents: "... lit by nine lotus-shaped chandeliers, with walls decorated with rich red and gold canvases in the chinoiserie style supported by painted dragons. The tall windows were dressed with opulent blue silk-satin draperies supported by carved flying dragons. The magnificent gilded domed ceiling was made up of hundreds of plaster cockleshells creating an illusion of height..."
"Thus giving the room its grandeur!" thought Henry, "and whoever decorated it did a wonderful job."
When he looked into the majestic gilded moulded mirror, something strange happened. He spotted a slight shimmer of mist reflecting in the glass. Slowly the room filled with a cloud of smoke, warping and twisting in front of him. From within the cloud he heard noises, the clinking of glasses, voices, and laughter, which was accompanied by strong smelling wafts of tobacco floating into the room, changing the mist into silver whirls of smoke curling through the air. Through the smoke, a blurred image of a group of people became visible. At first, the scene looked slightly out of focus. It was like a badly taken photograph but soon the images from past times matured into men dressed in period clothes, seated in luxurious gilded armchairs next to small round tables, smoking cigars. They replenished their tiny glasses with brandy, the merits and capabilities of

many heroes became the subject of animated discussion. The men were in the midst of an after-dinner gathering, and they appeared to be in good spirits. Henry watched the smoke floating through the room until it curled around the gilded dome, hanging below the pretty plaster ceiling roses. Irritated by the smoke, Henry blinked his eyes and instantly, the men and the smoke vanished, leaving him with an image of Georgian past times imprinted on his mind. The images he had seen had put a smile on his face, the palace seemed to hold some secret 'living' memories.

He took a bite of the chorizo and cheese skewer and mingled in with the other guests. The tour-guide entered the Music Room, where an elegantly dressed lady, who introduced herself as Vicky, invited the group to join her on the tour.
They entered the long corridor, linking the Music Room with the Banqueting Room, adorned with brightly-painted lanterns decorated with tassels, which served as an area for playing cards and musical entertainment. Vicky beckoned the group who followed her, passing the yellow imperial staircase, noticing its mahogany handrails carved as if to resemble bamboo. The upstairs gallery was dramatically lit by a large painted-glass laylight.

Vicky opened the door from the low ceilinged corridor to the Banqueting Room, and the participants were left dazzled by the change in scale and the splendour of its flamboyant decorations, and bold design. From the centre of the dome hung a huge thirty-foot chandelier, held in the claws of a silvered dragon, suspended from the apex of the ceiling; below it, six smaller silver dragons exhaled light through lotus glass shades. The room was furnished with lampshades, majestic fifteen foot high porcelain pagodas and original lamp stands. In the middle of the room, two armchairs and thirty plain chairs were displayed around a massive table with a lavish display of ormolu, candelabra, cutlery, and plates.
"King George IV had beautiful bright and spacious rooms, but he needed to recruit a couple of interior designers to turn this place into a flamboyant house with plenty of class, to be admired by his wealthy friends. Impulsively, he decided to send his most trusted courtiers to the Far East to purchase the most beautiful wallpapers and ceramics, ruby red and gold coloured curtains, and he commissioned two designers to make his romantic and fantastical visions a reality. As you can tell, George loved Chinese-inspired design and imagined the parlour in 'Chinoiserie' design."

Vicky opened the doors to the Banqueting Room Gallery, the site of the original farmhouse, with French windows opening onto a terrace, and palm tree columns supporting the upper floor.
At the same time, it seemed the doors at the end of the room opened as well. At first Henry couldn't believe his eyes. Pretty ladies dressed in silk gowns, and handsome gentlemen with fitted dress-coats entered the room. They danced in groups of two and four couples, forming a square, and took turns in dancing to the band playing piano, cornet, violin, and violoncello. During the dance the men and ladies exchanged partners and danced with different people. Henry was amused. He thoroughly enjoyed the music and watched the men and women dancing, taking turns, until he caught the eyes of a beautiful woman, and gracefully bowing he asked her whether she would give him the honour of joining him in a quadrille. She graciously accepted his invitation and whilst they danced, he appreciated the instrumental score. Whilst he made acquaintance with the beautiful woman, he heard footsteps, moving closer.
"Excuse me, Sir." Vicky tapped Henry on his shoulder.
Startled, the image of the beautiful woman he had just met faded away. "Oh dear, I must have ... but

what happened to the beautiful lady? I asked her to join me for a quadrille, and where are all the people who were dancing in this very same room?"
"Are you all right?" asked the guide. She looked at him with sympathetic concern. "I didn't see them, but I've been told the palace has been shrouded in mysteries since the king left. Some guests have told me they've seen ghost sightings of King George IV. Perhaps, you've witnessed one of them. George used to organise lavish balls under the chandeliers in this room. The guests were dressed in their finest and would be paired up to dance. This palace is a magical place with so many memories, and there's more to be explored. We're about to move on to the next room, the recently refurbished 'Saloon', please follow me." Vicky gave Henry a nod and smiled.
The group audibly gushed when they stepped into a room of spectacular luxuriousness with silver and 'pearl white' wall decorations, platinum leaves, crimson and gold silk panels and magnificent drapery. Vicky stood in front of the chimneypiece facing the group.
"This room, decorated for King George IV in 1823, was restored to the dazzling splendour of its original interior design, and it was re-opened to the public on 8th September 2018. The floor is fitted with a lavish circular carpet, a swirling kaleidoscope of

birds, dragons, sun rays, and lotus leaves."
On the gilded armchair, next to the chimneypiece, Henry spotted an exquisitely crafted red silk velvet robe, probably inspired by costumes worn at the Tudor and Stuart courts of the late sixteenth and seventeenth centuries, and, there was a handwritten note placed next to it.
This coronation robe worn by King George IV is going on show to the public for the first time in 30 years as part of a Regency fashion exhibition in Brighton.
Henry was overwhelmed with the beauty of it, and recovering from the shock, he sat down on the round velvet ottoman in the centre of the room. Vicky's voice faded away, and he drifted off.

A light reflected in the immense mirror hanging on the wall attracted Henry to look at it, and as he approached, he could see the surface rippling, and the reflection was no reflection at all. He could see an identical image of himself standing in a large gothic abbey church, dressed in the ermine coronation robe he had seen before, and the image held out its hand. At first Henry hesitated but, he drew closer and the pale hand came to him through the glistening surface, touching his hand. He saw images of the day George was crowned a king in Westminster Abbey, wearing the same robe with a

long red velvet train decorated with embroidered gold stars - so long that it had to be carried by eight pages. The icing on the cake was an elaborate coronation crown, decorated with over 12,000 sparkling diamonds, making it one of the most extravagant coronations in history. He saw an image of Hyde Park, the 'lungs of London', where he used to go for a stroll. It was followed by visions of a regatta and boat race on the 'Serpentine', a canal flowing through Hyde Park, with illuminations of coloured Chinese lanterns and a grand firework display. He was sure this vision must be connected to the coronation of George IV.
His eyes searched the room, as if he had seen something, sensing a presence. In the far distance, he vaguely heard a loud sound similar to that of a horn of a ship. He focused on the bright, piercing and stately sound echoing outside through the air and, instead of a ship's horn, he realised it was the sound of trumpet, heralding the entrance of a monarch. The room looked blurred, a slight shimmer of mist appeared in front of him, quickly filling up the room turning into a cloud. It was being warped and twisted in front of him, changing the space into a charming room with the most impressive paintings with shining gilded frames, exquisite floral wallpaper, and a magnificent carpet

stretching across the floor. The only piece of furniture in the room was a gold throne, crested with a coat of arms supported by a yellow lion and a white unicorn.
Henry heard the sound of muffled footsteps, rustling silk, and he smelt the sweet fragrance of bergamot and mandarin lingering in the air. Could it be there was someone else in the room? But where? He looked back into the mirror and saw the faint reflection of a man with fine brown hair, resting his right hand beside the Imperial Crown on a round occasional table. Captivated by this intriguing image he stepped closer, Henry was moving towards the mirror, but as soon as his fingers touched it, a crack appeared running across the glass. The man had disappeared and Henry looked at the distorted image of himself, a spitting image of the other man. He ran his index finger over the frame, touched its cool ridges and grooves, and the layer of dust that clung to it. He was lost in thoughts. About King George. He was even more sure of his convictions.

Henry woke up on the King's bed. Looking at his sleeve, he noticed his shirt was different, and not only his shirt, also his trousers, his shoes, and to his surprise he was even wearing a waistcoat. He took the heavy robe from the chair placed next to the bed, ran his hands over the soft fabric, and held it up. It was as clean as the day it was created and just as supple, just as beautiful.

The sound of footsteps in the corridor attracted Henry's attention. The footsteps stopped outside the bedroom followed by a knock at the door.

"Who's there?" Henry asked with a slightly high pitched concerned voice.

"Your majesty, it's only me, Charles, your Gentleman of the bedchamber. I've brought you your nightshirt, and a bowl filled with water and fresh towels."

Deryk

On a hot and sweltering summer day, I took a well-deserved break, and paid a visit to Godstone, a village in the hills of Surrey. I was told it attracted many visitors and soon found out why it was so popular. The village was built along a busy stretch of the London to Brighton Roman road, and had plenty of inns attracting traders to spend the night: it was a goldmine. The reason why I mention this village is because it's very close to my heart. It's where I met a farmer at the Hare and Hounds Inn. His name was John, and from the moment we talked, we got on really well. After a beer he found out it was my first visit to Godstone and kindly offered me a tour of the village and, impressed as I was by his appearance and kindness, I gratefully accepted his offer.
We walked through the streets and he explained Godstone was divided in two parts, Godstone Green and Church Town. Church Town was a quiet area with old timber framed buildings, dominated by St Nicholas Church, whilst Godstone Green had thrived on the busy thoroughfare. Increasing numbers of wagons, coaches and all kinds of travellers from far and beyond had encouraged the establishment of many inns like the cosy Hare and Hounds, and the Rose and Crown built next

door to the Bell Inn.
We walked along the pretty ponds admiring the wind mills, trees and meadows. The pond was busy with wagoneers driving their tired horses down its gently sloping bank to be watered.
We played horseshoes, a game in which two adult men tossed iron 'u' shaped horseshoes at iron pegs set in the ground. There was no shortage of old horseshoes as they tend to come loose after a month or so, and have to be replaced by the farriers on a daily basis when the guests stayed overnight at the inns..
"Have you ever seen an iron horseshoe hanging above the front door of a house near the sea?" John asked. "Up here, it's quite common. Do you know the story behind it?"
I shrugged my shoulders. "I don't, but I'm eager to hear your story."
"Well, let me explain. The story behind the custom of hanging horseshoes above doors, goes all the way back to ancient times. It all has to do with luck.
There was once a blacksmith called Dunstan who lived in Sussex. He later became a famous saint. One day the devil visited him and demanded shoes for his hoofed feet. Dunstan nailed a red hot horseshoe right onto his foot. When the devil screamed in pain and begged him to take it off, Dunstan only agreed to remove it after the devil promised to respect the sign of the horseshoe and never to

pass under any lintel where it hung.
The tradition carried on, and people added onto to the legend of the horseshoe. It is said that witches are afraid of horses and their iron shoes. People thought that witches would never pass through a doorway with one hung above it, but I guess, they were superstitious. Nowadays, hanging a horseshoe facing upwards in a 'U' shape is said to keep evil out and bring good luck into your home."
"That's a fascinating story. I guess I need to take one back home with me and place it above the entrance of The Black Lion, and hopefully it will bring good luck."
"Oh, I must tell you, Godstone is known to have a witch, she's named Polly Paine, and she can turn herself into both a cat and a hare. I've seen it with my own eyes. I witnessed a pack of hounds give chase to a hare which fled to Polly Paine's cottage. Then it jumped down into Stratton Brook, although it had been badly bitten by one if the dogs on its hind leg. But then, the hare just disappeared!"
"She must have been very scared." I said. "There are witches where I live, and their brews appear to have healing powers. It's probably why people believe they are different to the others. They are often used as a scapegoat when things go wrong, being blamed for a bad harvest, destructive storms, bursting river banks. I think it is tragic that so many of the accused were found guilty."

"I guess you're right, Deryk, and I hope I'll be able to travel down south and meet a witch who can help me to recover from my aches and pains." John smiled and suggested having another drink at the nearby White Hart Inn.

From the moment we walked in, it felt warm and inviting, with old wooden beams and pillars, wood burning stoves and a roaring open fire with an inglenook. It was a very cosy place, and over a beer and a good old chat, John told me the local pubs had beer gardens which opened during the summer, log fires during the winter, and beer festivals on draught. Jokingly he suggested I should move up here to open another inn. I liked his idea, the place definitely had a rich history of hop growing and strong links to the brewing industry and was situated on a busy junction where lots of people would stop and spend the night. But, I was relieved to know he fully understood I couldn't take up his suggestion as my trade was at Brighthelmstone where I ran the brewery and inn.

They say a few drinks will loosen someone's tongue, and slowly the subject changed to travelling over land and seas, and eventually, we started talking about our professions and our lives. We were having a good time, but after a few more beers, and totally out of the blue, John opened up about his personal life.

"There are such stereotypes about farmers that it's

always expected that you get married, have children, settle down on the farm. These days, that's what life entails as a farmer."

"What do you mean by that? We're all expected to get married, have children and live your life."

"I struggle with hiding my secret because I fear I would be considered too weak by those around me to work with animals, if the truth came out."

"Who would consider you to be too weak? I think you're a strong man, running a farm, herding the sheep, the outdoor life can be very tough, with forever-changing weather conditions. I don't know how you do it, but I admire you. If I can help, please tell me. You can confide in me. It sounds like you have reached the point that your secret has become unbearable."

"It was difficult for me growing up, and there's no road map to do this kind of thing, but to be honest, I think I fancy men more than I do women. There you go, I've just let the cat out of the bag. Can you imagine a farmer without a wife, farming the land with a man? People would laugh, wouldn't they?"

"That's a very brave confession to make. I can empathise and it must have been very difficult for you growing up, but you're right, there's no road map to do this kind of thing. I guess you must have suffered?"

"Looking back, I definitely have been suffering quite a bit, and then it just dawned on me, a sudden realisation,

that it just has to happen. Not only for myself but for the people around me whom I love and who love me back, to be true to them really. I knew that the person who had the biggest problem with it was myself and, I don't know how to thank you for letting me talk. You seem to be very accepting."
There was a silence, I thought it would be inappropriate to respond, and I'm glad I didn't as he continued.
"I don't know, but you seem different. I just knew I could talk to you. No one here understands. I was struggling, until today, until I met you. Farming is a difficult business at the best of times. It's isolated, tough, prone to animal diseases, people are poor.
"If we have any riches, it's in the form of our animals. Any money we manage to scrimp together and save has to be spent on rent, food and animal fodder. In the freezing winter, a farmer rises long before dawn to care for the sheep or cattle, out in all weathers to look after the flocks and crops - and often we're famished and cold."
John didn't have much money and had lived here all his life. Although his wife had been great, he knew from throughout his years of growing up that trying to find the life partner in Godstone he really wanted was like finding a needle in a haystack. And then there was me, living in Brighthelmstone, the town where everything was possible. I empathised with his tough life as a farmer, and invited him to come down and visit me one day at the

brewery and inn. It seemed that he was willing to travel down to Brighthelmstone whenever he could. We raised our glasses, finished our drinks and headed back to his house where there was a horseshoe hanging above the front door.
John introduced me to his wife, Jane, and she told me everything was farmed by hand. Their house was named 'Godstone Farm' and they worked from early morning till the evening on the land of William Clayton, who was the Lord of the Manor of Godstone and Bletchingley. It had a small stream called Stratton Brook running through the estate, which was, from what I remembered, an escape route for witches.

Later, after John had promised to visit me in Brighthelmstone, I kissed him and his wife goodbye and I whispered in his ear, "Your secret sits silently in both our hearts."
He winked at me as I mounted my horse, we waved goodbye, and I followed the narrow country road set in ancient woodlands fringing the old road and village of Godstone. When I approached the tiny bridged stream, I heard something rustling through the trees. Looking sideways I couldn't see anything, except for the swaying fronds of the large ferns. I narrowed my eyes and then I saw a lady with a white bonnet, looking behind her, as if fearing for her life. When she saw me, she fled, holding

her dress pulled up to her knees, running into one of the cottages. When I passed it, I read the name on the name plate on the gate, 'Polly Paine's Cottage'.

Booking Eight

Sharon and Paul resided in Edinburgh, a magical city full of ancient buildings, hidden closes and underground vaults creating a mystical atmosphere. It was a city of enchanting and stunning landscapes. Sharon was the Chef de Cuisine at The Witchery, a restaurant situated near the gates of Edinburgh Castle; and Paul, a tour-guide at Mary King's Close, took people to the narrow streets of tenement houses hidden underneath the buildings on the Royal Mile. After it was closed to the public for many years, the area became shrouded in myths and urban legends. Tales of hauntings and murders abounded until it reopened, when Mary King's Close became a popular visitor's attraction. Paul and Sharon met when they became followers of white witchcraft, also known as Wicca, and soon they vowed to love, honour, respect and protect each other in a hand-fasting ceremony in the vaults below Niddry Street in the old town of Edinburgh.

Paul and Sharon wanted to explore the past and left Edinburgh at the crack of dawn to go on their honeymoon in Southern England. They chose this destination because it was a region of old pilgrimage routes, holy wells, and ancient churches, forming a matrix of sacred sites: the last refuge of Paganism before Christianity became widespread over all of England.

Very late in the afternoon they arrived by car in Chiddingly, a picturesque village in East Sussex founded on seven hills, surrounded by beautiful countryside with trees and plenty of little woods. Sharon had read that the old church was crowned by a stone spire of 128 feet added in the fifteenth century, bearing the name 'Pelham Buckle', the badge of the family who were lords of the manor of Laughton, and the Six Bells Inn opposite the church, was named after the peal of bells found in the church tower.

For their first visit Sharon had booked a magical escape, a large yurt idyllically set in the shady woods: and it was simply perfect. The king-sized bed was covered with a pale green quilt with a lovely paisley print in shades of cream, orange, red and green. There was a wood burning stove in case the nights should get cooler, and lots of candles they could light which would make the yurt feel romantic. It reminded Paul and Sharon of when they held hands in the middle of a circle of candles.

Outside there was a cast-iron pot to cook food on a barbecue or alternatively, there were a few local pubs, all within walking distance.
After a cup of green tea, they decided to go out for a walk, looking for a local pub.
The silvery moon was shining over the dark woods, which seemed to be whispering in the evening, and Paul and Sharon were nearing the great Wealden Forest, standing on marshy grounds where now Willetts Stream divides Chiddingly from Muddles Green. Beyond it was the line of the Downs and the ghostly outline of the Long Man of Wilmington. Locals held on to the theory of ley-lines, those mysterious lines of force connecting ancient sacred sites, suggesting there was such a line running north from the Long Man through the churchyard.
Paul and Sharon continued their walk through the woods until they reached a main road where they saw an old pub with glowing wall lanterns. It was the Six Bells Inn, situated next to the old sandstone church. Paul and Sharon, attracted by the ancient church, crossed the road and entered the churchyard. It was filled with rows of silent tombstones and dramatically embossed graves to the left and right. It was like a sea of the dead. Some were crumbled with the weathering of centuries, some were smooth marble with new black writing

and laid with floral tributes. Most though, were overgrown and unkept, for now probably even their mourners had joined them under the clay soil.
"Luckily I brought my torch with me." Paul smiled at Sharon.
'I'm so glad you did. The moonlight does help to see things, but we do need light to see all the details." She looked around her. "What's that over there? Paul, could you point the torch towards the church wall please?"
Paul and Sharon walked over to the wall. The bright torch light revealed a set of grey, broken tomb stones engraved with holy crosses and fragments of names, all piled up together.
"It looks like someone just dumped them here, how disgraceful!" Paul kneeled down in front of the pile of debris to examine the stones. "Look, there's soil on this tomb stone, it feels moist."
"It smells like it's been dug out recently," said Sharon.
Paul moved closer and looked at the inscriptions and the dates.
"I don't like to see graves disturbed," said Sharon. "But maybe the church authorities are just re-organising the graveyard. They need maintenance like this sometimes, I've heard. But I still don't like to see the dead disturbed like this!"

"Oh?" said Paul, a hint of enquiry in his tone. "But you must know, darling, that there are certain powerful rituals you can achieve through ... well, let's not talk about it now. We can talk later..."
At the same moment, they heard a loud clanging coming from the church tower and it rolled through the village as if it were thunder.
Sharon's heart beat fast at the sound of the bells. "Blimey! That took me by surprise. It's quite loud, isn't it? I thought for one second my heart would stop beating."
She grabbed Paul's hand, but as he felt her pulse he noticed it was very low. "Sharon, are you ok? You feel very cold?"
Her strong grip became tighter. As it did, the sound of the church bells grew louder too. Instead of Sharon, it was a man's hand he was holding. How could that be? He looked into the eyes of the man that had replaced his wife and started to scream. Quickly, he tried to free himself. "Let me go! Hey, let me go, I said!"
A voice resounded in his head. He was sure it was the man speaking although his mouth remained closed.
'Leave this place!'
"This is crazy, I can hear your voice in my head. Just let me go," Paul begged.

'Leave this place and I promise I'll let you go! Yesterday the bells were ringing at your ceremony but today, the church bells ring for me. It was in the belfry tower where my body once lay after being exhumed. Every year, in January, the church bells will ring until to dust I return. I beg you, please take my word and go! You're in grave danger!'

Abruptly, Paul's hand was freed. There were hands on his arms now.

"Let me go!" Paul continued.

"Paul, it's me!" said Sharon.

"Sharon?" He blinked in disbelief. "You're here?"

"Of course I'm here, where else would I be?"

"But… but… just now, there was a man."

"A man? What are you talking about?"

"Instead of you, there was a man. Exactly where you're standing. Did you not hear me scream?"

"No. I heard nothing. One minute we were holding hands, the next you got that look on your face, as if you'd blacked out."

"Blacked out?" Is that what had happened? Had he imagined the entire incident with that strange man? It was the only thing that made sense. These black outs, sometimes they happened to him. The doctor had referred him for tests. He shook his head.

"You're right, it must have been a blackout. Thank goodness you were here."

"I'm not surprised you were unconscious for a minute or so. You've hardly eaten all day. Luckily I brought this lovely cheese and onion pie with me, all freshly cooked by yours truly." Sharon opened her handbag and showed Paul the mouthwatering pie. "I hid it in the cool-box during our journey in the back of the car. Be a good boy and eat it all up!"
Paul tucked into the pie and after he had finished it, he said, "Thank you, that was tasty, but I'm thirsty now. Shall we go for that drink in the pub? It may still be open."
"Yes, darling, that sounds like a great idea. After all, cheese does make people thirsty, doesn't it? Let's go and get you a drink quickly."
When they walked towards the pub, Paul started to feel unwell. "My stomach, I think I'm going to be sick."
"Quick, into the woods with you!" Sharon witnessed Paul rushing towards the trees, breathing the cool air rapidly. The darkness pressed in on him. Then he felt an excruciating pain inside his stomach. It felt like a fire rushing through his veins. Kneeling down on the damp earth, holding his stomach with his hands, he instinctively knew something was very wrong. It must have been the cheese and onion pie. He had trusted Sharon, but instead he was pushed blindly into the dark forest where she had revealed

her true and dark side by using the forbidden powers of malicious black magic to poison him. He should have taken the man's word that he was in grave danger, but it was too late now, and within seconds he collapsed.

Sharon looked at her watch, it was coming up to 10 pm. She sighed and took a deep breath, shaking her head as if to rid herself of the clinging horror of what had just happened.
She felt drained after the events of the last half an hour. When she saw the light of the lanterns hanging outside the Six Bells Inn, she longed to go in and get herself a drink. Common sense dictated that she kept out of sight, but emotional exhaustion was causing her legs to buckle at the knees. She made her way to the deserted benches outside the pub and sat down beneath an open window. Through the window, she could hear that local musicians were playing their songs and one was beginning an acoustic version of *'Moonlight Shadow'*, prompted by the beautiful red Hunters Moon, which had been very conspicuous in the clear skies for the past few nights. The song had a catchy melody, the kind of song you want to sing sitting around a campfire. Tonight it was the first time she really listened to its lyrics, and, ironically, the piece was

about a woman helplessly witnessing the violent and unexpected death of her lover. After the singer had finished the song, he got a round of applause. Then she overheard a conversation between two men standing near the open window.
"Did you hear that Sarah has been taken to the Hellingly Centre today? She's staying at Willow Ward. I've been told she is likely to be detained for life."
"Poor Bill. Never understood how he managed to put up with her. She is as mad as a hatter!"
"Would you travel to France every week because your wife wants cheaper ingredients for her pie-business? You must be kidding me!"
"I don't think he had much choice. He had no job and he was helping her out as everything was so much cheaper over there. A fiver for a large sack of onions and a tenner for a bucket load of meat. It's a no-brainer, isn't it?"
"Sounds like big business to me. After he passed away people in the village were talking about his sudden death, and rumours were he died of arsenic poisoning."
"I do wonder how she managed to administer it into his favourite supper without him knowing?"
"Well, this is between you and me, but I've been told Bill bought the arsenic himself from a shop in

Horsebridge. It was to kill mice in their house. He gave the arsenic to Sarah to put it away in a safe place where no one else could find it. On Christmas Eve she served him his favourite cheese and onion pie, and after a few days, Bill started to feel ill. His breath smelt of garlic, he had terrible stomach cramps, and his hair started to fall out. He went into a coma and died the following week. After Bill died, Sarah started a relationship with Elliott who lived just opposite her. Soon people put two and two together. Apparently she'd been shagging her Elliott for months before Bill's death and she told people she wanted to marry him."

"Terrible, isn't it? Bill was such a nice guy. Always happy to help. He arranged the ingredients of his own death without realising it."

Sharon smiled slightly to herself as she watched the big red moon shining bright and long in the sky. The local singer began singing 'The Witch's Promise'. She listened to the lyrics, which he sang so beautifully with his high tenor voice. It felt like everyone knew about what happened in the woods, even the lyrics were a dark reference to the woods and her ruthless act, but she had no other choice. These people could not know what she knew. Sharon quickly rose from the cold bench and moved off into the darkness.

When she arrived back at the yurt she found a newspaper on the table. 'Where did that come from?' She had not seen it before and picked it up. It was an edition of the Historic Sussex dated 11th April 1852. It was quite old, and she wondered how it had ended up here. She opened it and inside she saw a story with the headline *The truth behind Cheese and Onion Pie Murder*. After the two songs she heard in the pub, clearly making a reference to what happened earlier that evening, this seemed to be another reference - it couldn't be true! She tried to remember if it had been there before they left. She read the article.

After William French's burial took place on 27th January 1852, evidence came to light against Sarah Ann French, a regular of the Six Bells Inn, and her possible involvement in her husband's death which led to an inquest to further investigate. Coroner Alfrid Swayn Taylor found a number of small yellow patches on his body, and came to the conclusion it was arsenic poisoning. Sarah was found guilty for the wilful murder of her husband William French and she was the last female to be hanged at Lewes prison for her crime. Several people visiting the graveyard, have witnessed William's spirit haunting the church grounds, warning newly wed husbands to flee the town before it's too late.

It made her think about what Paul had said. He was convinced he had seen a man where she was standing, but despite Sharon's powers, the ghost only appeared to him. But Paul had friends, dangerous friends. Were they communicating via this paper - and if so, how had they moved so fast? She pondered things for a while, thinking of the long-ago Sarah French and her death. After a while, she put the paper back on the table and looked at her watch. It was almost midnight, it was time to go to sleep. Just when she wanted to jump into her night gear, Sharon's phone beeped. It was an email from Sarah. She tossed her full long brown hair over her shoulder, and paused before sending a response.

Hi lovely.
Just wanted to say I hope you're OK - and thanks for that pie recipe. It went down a treat! Looking forward to visiting you in a couple of days in the Hellingly Centre.
Love, your little sis xxx

That was all she dared to write, knowing that anything she told Sarah would be intercepted. She hoped they would have a chance to converse privately and then she would be able to tell her the story of tonight: how she had seen an ambulance arriving as she left the pub and had bumped into a local woman who told her a man walking his dog late at night had found a lifeless body behind the trees.

"Nobody saw us arrive together," Sharon told herself, "and the yurt belongs to Sarah. Nobody can trace us to it. It's amazing that mum kept our great-great-great-grandmother's cookery book up in her attic. Why is it that history always repeats itself?"

When she had pressed the send button, she opened the door and watched the charcoal sky. In the distant hills, she heard the thunder rolling across the malevolent sky, its power echoing across the woods. Without waiting for the coming storm to break, she headed towards her car when her eye caught dozens of flickering lights, moving slowly through the trees. She could hear noises, children giggling, adults talking, some were singing a tune. Sharon moved closer and saw dozens of children and adults were holding paper lanterns, following the paths through the woods. It was the local children's midnight lantern parade. It looked like a twinkling procession.

The thunder rolled overhead like the fury of the gods, tumbling towards her through the dark clouds, spreading out over the hills, the squall coming her way. She walked back towards her car, and decided it would be better to find a safe place elsewhere, a house rather than a tent, protecting her from the worse to come. She sat down in the car seat, looked into the rear-view mirror, and removed the mysterious pendant which she kept around her neck. She looked at the mirror and her true self, a sign of her frailty, seeing herself at her most vulnerable moment. There certainly was magic in the stone: it allowed her to keep the glamour of a young woman, instead of an old one. She may be old, but her spells were still working, and she proved herself lucky with her younger and trustworthy sister Sarah. The day before her wedding in Edinburgh Sarah had texted her, and warned her that she had found out Paul belonged to a secret and dark society, just like her sister's late husband. The society believed in the active existence of the devil and wanted to use demons as evil forces to possess and cause harm to men and women. Their aim was to put witchcraft and witches in league with the devil.

When the sisters had realised this, they knew that their sworn task as white witches was to fight this evil, for they were part of an ancient witch lineage which worked in secret against demonic powers. For the first time, they had been forced to reveal their darkest sides, eliminating their lovers who had

become their enemies. History had indeed repeated itself: their ancestor, Sarah French, had had to murder her husband William for the same reason, more than one hundred and fifty years before.
Her phone beeped, a new email had arrived. She tapped the envelope with her finger, and a message opened.

Hi Sharon,

My apologies for the late response. I've been away on holiday and only just found your email. I know it's a little bit late but I wanted to let you know the Black Lion Cottage is available from tonight. You can pop around at anytime. Regards, Matt

She turned the key, started the car, and followed the roads over the cliffs heading to Brighton. A special place where witchcraft was now a new religion being practised by a coven of white witches living in a cottage called 'The Witch Ball', perched in the centre of the Lanes area, an easy place to miss on a meander, but a real treasure trove once found.

Deryk

On a dark and stormy evening, back in October 1554, a small group of men all the way from the county of Surrey arrived at The Black Lion. They were drenched to the skin. I was expecting them and invited them in. Whilst they were looked after by the bartenders, one of my members of staff walked their horses to the backyard, providing them with some shelter from the rain, removed the saddles, and made sure there was plenty of hay and water in the trough. Inside the inn I had joined the group of men, and the warmth radiating from the lamps and chandelier was comforting for them. Their clothes were put over the benches, drying in front of the brick hearth at the far end of the room. Then I saw him, standing in the middle of the group: John Launder. Our eyes met again, and we needed no words. The good-looking man had kept his promise, and had come down south to visit me.

John was joined by his friend Thomas Iveson, a carpenter also from Godstone, and had travelled on account of his father's business. Upon their arrival, having heard that I was a man that 'did much favour the Gospel', they resorted to my house to seek my company. John had told Thomas that I was a brewer and my place of work was in Black Lion Street. Officially John and Thomas were here to discuss the possibility of stocking my beers in their local pubs, but the real reason they were here was to read from the Luther Bible and the Book of Gospels, together with the other men who had come down here. I told everyone that the Sheriff recently visited me, and that he enquired whether I knew anything about readings taking place in this town. Allegedly someone had told him that she believed she had seen the forbidden book circulating in houses and shops, and ever since, he had been keeping a close eye on me. I insisted that all the men had to remain discreet about our meeting tonight, nobody must know about it as anyone reading from the Luther Bible, or even listening to it, could face imprisonment, and even being hanged, drawn and quartered. There were several more men who arrived that night and everyone swore to me that their lips would be sealed. My wife and the bartenders looked after everyone and the beer proved to be very popular amongst my new friends. Later that evening, in the cellars, we read from the book and read out loud some of the prayers. Upstairs, the inn was filled with people drinking, singing, telling each other jokes, and I could hear them laughing out loud.

It was past midnight. The guests and the group of men had left, except John and Thomas who stayed for the night. I had gone to my private room and John had

joined me. He told me he was mesmerised by the words I read from my book, and perhaps, he was mesmerised by me as well? After some more reading we became tired, and went to sleep.
That same night, Edward Cage, the Sussex Sheriff, an official responsible for keeping the peace throughout the county on behalf of the Queen, broke into the upstairs room of the brewery, where he found John and me and the Book of Gospels, written in English, which was forbidden in the time of Queen Mary. The poor lad had travelled to the wrong place at the wrong time.
John and I were arrested, and the same night we were sent to Newgate Prison in London. We were driven in a four-wheeled carriage pulled by the Sheriff's horses over the muddy and slippery roads, braving howling gales and torrential rain. The horse and carriage took us to Hassocks from where we crossed the South Downs, passing through Felbridge and Godstone in the North Downs. From there we followed the hilly flint and sandstone roads until, a day later, we arrived in London, a place of many workshops of craftsmen and traders. Nearly every road and street had shops and iron mongers, and I could also see that many properties lined the street across London Bridge. What I saw was unbelievable. On the bridge were many buildings, some standing up to five storeys high. Some overhung the road, forming a dark tunnel through which we passed. The

horses trotted through the narrow muddy streets lined with tall dark buildings, and looking around me, I watched the foul streets, wet from water spillages by water carriers who regularly went around the streets with their packhorses selling water to the householders. The constant smell of mud and horse manure was everywhere, dogs' urine and men's too, dregs of beer and cast-off bits of fish, and other filth. The city counted over a hundred churches with tall spires and towers, with St Paul's the most impressive.

The horses took us through Cheapside where we passed the poultry dealers and a corn market which was held in a churchyard, leading to Newgate Street, used by butchers for slaughterhouses and stalls. The horses stopped in front of the entrance of Newgate Prison, the most notorious prison in London. It is almost impossible to describe the terror in my mind, when I was first brought in. I heard the piercing and terrifying screams of inmates, smelled the unbearable stench lingering around me, and was almost overcome by the bad atmosphere. Through the long journey, John had been with me, which was of great comfort but now we had entered the pit of hell, the underworld of London.

Booking Nine

Rick, born in Bristol, achieved his bachelor's degree in finance and became a venture capitalist. He became bored with investing in companies and looked around for something more creative and meaningful to him. At a charity event, he met a legendary lyricist, known for his work on some celebrated musicals, and this inspired him to invest in theatre. Shows needed money, and Rick loved musicals and stage shows. It seemed to him a perfect match and he started to invest in theatre productions in Chichester and London. Frequently attending event launch parties accompanied by glamorous escorts, Rick claimed that he owed his success in life to his belief in the motto 'carpe diem', enjoying the pleasures of the moment without concern for the future. One morning he had planned a meeting to discuss an exciting investment opportunity in premier multi-arts venue Brighton Dome and booked a cottage near the venue to spend the night.

The journey from Chichester was delayed due to a broken-down train, and Rick arrived at the cottage slightly later than planned. There was still plenty of time left to get himself ready to join the ghost walk in Lewes. It was part of his research, as he wanted to know everything about the medieval town for a new stage production about the plague which struck the town during the reign of Mary in the sixteenth century. He took a quick shower, ordered a taxi, and after a swift twenty minute taxi-journey the driver dropped him off in the High Street. It was a quiet midweek evening with few people around, but on top of the hill, he saw a group of people standing in front of the war memorial at the junction of High Street and Market Street. It was a bronze obelisk with three winged bronze statues. The statue of Victory was standing on the top of a globe, facing east towards Flanders. On the west face was seated the statue of Liberty holding a torch, and on the east face was a similar figure of Peace with a dove on her left shoulder, her right arm holding a wreathed bronze shield. In the centre of the group of people stood a mysterious-looking man dressed in a black cape. He was wearing a top hat and holding a walking stick topped with a ghoulish skull. Rick attracted the attention of the mysterious man, who smiled at him as he raised his cape, spreading it with bat-like wings, and greeted the crowd of people. "Welcome to the haunted Lewes Ghost Walk! Ever

since I've lived here, I have seen and heard things I can't explain. When all other explanations have been explored, you must be left with the truth: that there is life after death, and sometimes these two worlds meet. Lewes has been the site of burnings, murders, plagues and ghost sightings, dating back through many centuries, and it's rumoured that even Jack the Ripper had connections here." The crowd looked at the man in astonishment.
"During this walk we will encounter the dark side of Lewes, a fascinating journey through the streets, graveyards, and alleyways of this ancient market town. A place where a legion of lost souls have been haunting the streets and are dying to make your acquaintance. Right here, we're standing at the War Memorial in the middle of the road, an example of a place traditionally associated with lost souls. Many strangers visiting the town often think that the spot itself has something to do with the war, but they couldn't be more mistaken. It marks the spot where Protestants were burned to death when Catholic Mary was Queen. Most of them imprisoned in the cellars of the Town Hall to await their gruesome fate. Every year the town organises an event called 'Bonfire Night' held on 5th November commemorating the foiled Guy Fawkes's gunpowder plot, but it also commemorates the memory of the

seventeen Protestant Martyrs burned right here at the War Memorial. Each year, seventeen flaming crosses are paraded through the streets in commemoration of the martyrs and effigies are wheeled through the town before being burnt on the enormous bonfires on the outskirts. Lewes has been keeping up this tradition for many centuries. Tonight, there are more dark things to be explored, but before we start the ghost walk, I would like to take you back to the sixteenth century."

The man beckoned the group to follow him.

They crossed the dimly lit road and stopped in front of a red brick building with three arches.

"In the sixteenth century, due to the decline in Lewes Castle, seventeen martyrs were imprisoned in the vaults below this pavement."

He pointed his finger to a plaque on the wall. "In 2016, as part of the renovation of the Lewes Town Hall façade, it was decided to create a hole in the pavement on the High Street, to allow people to see the steps associated so closely with the story of the martyrs, as told on this plaque. Through the glass panel you can see the original steps to the cellar of the old Star Inn, the same steps all martyrs would have walked up on their way to the stake, and now they have been opened up for public view."

Rick rested his hands on the railings and peered

through the glass. He spotted something lying on the steps: it looked like an old hat. He bent over to have a closer look. Then Rick's body felt strangely heavy, he felt dizzy, he didn't understand what was happening to him. Just when he wanted to ask somebody for help, he lost his balance and his body collapsed.

Rick opened his eyes and found himself lying on the floor at the bottom of the steps of the cellar, the silvery moon shining through the hole above him. The panel was cracked: it seemed he had fallen through it and when he looked around him he saw shattered pieces of glass all around. He sat up and inspected his arms and hands, they were covered in cuts and bruises. His head hurt terribly, and he had no recollection of what had happened. Alongside the shattered glass, the floor was covered with broken beer barrels, most of their wooden staves cracked. Outside he heard a man shouting, followed by the sound of a cart clattering over the cobbled street and trotting hooves. The last sound he heard was that of a barking dog, and then nothing.
The silence was broken by a soft object, gently toppling down the steps, ending up on the floor right in front of him. It was an old black, medieval-looking hat. He lay still, gazing at the hat, feeling too

dazed to move. But then he noticed a shadow obscuring the moonlight. He looked up and saw someone descending the steps. A cold sweat sprang up all over his body. His heart was racing as a hand brushed his hands, and he sensed the soft breath of someone near his mouth. Firmly, he gripped the hands. They were cold, large and hairy, revealing they belonged to a man. The man looked young, perhaps in his mid twenties, and was dressed in a long dark cloak from top to toe. Courteously the man stepped back and spoke with a hoarse voice which sounded like an old man, even though his face looked young.

'Please, don't be afraid, I mean no harm, there's not been a soul down here ever since I started guarding this doomed undercroft. After you spotted the hat, I saw you falling down the steps and was worried, so I walked down and touched your hand to check your pulse, and put my ear close to your mouth to check whether you were still breathing. You seemed to be fine.'

The man helped Rick to sit up, picked up the medieval hat, and looked into his eyes.

'I was imprisoned down here with my friend, awaiting our fate. Then, one morning, outside the Star Inn, I witnessed my friend being put into a barrel, and burning torches set the stake and his body alight. When he threw his arms up in the air and screamed, I fell down to my

knees in tears, and I thought this would be the moment he would die. But then he turned his face to me whilst the flames were licking the barrel and his body, and he said:
'Wait for me,
One day I will return,
I will find you ...'
These were the last words I heard coming from his mouth before I watched him becoming one with the flames and rise with the smoke above the streets of Lewes.
'Since then I've been guarding this place, and many centuries have passed but my spirit is still here, trapped, in a dimly lit parallel world within your world, and I haven't encountered my friend's spirit. Could it be, after all this time, his spirit is still around? Perhaps somewhere in your world?'
Rick felt so sorry for this spirit man and instead of being scared, he wanted to help him. "That's entirely possible, especially after such a gruesome death, his spirit may not have been able to find peace." Rick took the hat, turned it around, and saw two initials embroidered on the inside, D.C. He put it on his head and it fitted perfectly. From the moment he put it on, images appeared in his mind. At first they were blurred, but soon they started to become clear: visions of horses trotting on track roads; an old pub with a wrought iron chandelier and a hearth; prison bars and a massive church hall. He took it off, and as

he expected, the visions stopped. “I saw strange visions from past times, like a pub with a chandelier, men, and a hearth.”
‘*You could see his past by the hat. It was Deryk’s, he left it here before he was burned at the stake, and as far as I know, it’s all that’s left of him.*’
“You told me about Deryk’s fate, but what about yours? What happened to you after Deryk was burned?”

‘*It was as gruesome,*’ *said the spirit.* As he spoke, it seemed perfectly natural for Rick to be sitting in the moonlit cellar, listening to this ancient story of suffering and courage, and he gave all his attention to the young man with the hoarse voice.
The speaker continued, *‘but let me tell the story from the beginning. Deryk was a brewer, born in Flanders, and I was a farmer from Godstone in Surrey. I got married, dedicating my life to my wife and my work, constantly battling an inner fight I could not win. I became a tired man who no longer cared, and I was slowly turning into a bitter man. You probably won’t know, but at that time, England was officially a Roman Catholic country. Queen Mary had restored the old religion, and people travelled from one town to another to spread the latest news and gossip. One day, I met Deryk, the owner of a famous brewery and inn. I bumped*

into him in my hometown of Godstone, offered him a tour through the old town, and we became friends, very good friends. He met my wife, we had an evening roast, and he spent the night. The following day, before his departure, he insisted I should visit him at his brewery and inn to return the favour.

'At the end of October 1554, my friend Thomas and I travelled down to Brighthelmstone where I met Deryk for the second time. He was a handsome man with piercing hazel eyes, a black moustache and a beard. His charming appearance and looks attracted everyone, both women and men. Soon he told me about the meeting he had planned: and had invited a group of men to meet secretly in the cellars below the brewery and inn, where he would read gospels from the Luther Bible and perform a service in English. Both of these activities were strictly forbidden during the Queen's reign. After the meeting had finished, Deryk asked me to stay, and sent all the men upstairs to have a tankard of beer. When we first met in my hometown, I opened up to him about my struggles: I seemed to love men and women alike. Now it was Deryk's turn to tell me what he had on his mind. He told me he was devoted to his hard-working wife, just like me, but confessed he had unwillingly wed her, and wanted to share a secret with me he had never ever shared with anyone before. Back in the days in Flanders he had been happy; and he still was, but not as contented as he used to

be so I asked him what would content him? He said, despite being married, he had a secret desire he could only disclose to me, as he trusted me. Deryk said he showed an interest in both men and women, and had been thinking about whether he loved men more. If I was interested, he would read to me again from the book in private; and eager to get to know him better, I accepted his invitation. He entered the inn, told the men he felt tired and urged everyone to carry on drinking until the barrel ran dry.

We ascended the stairs and spent the rest of the evening in the upstairs room where Deryk read from his books, and afterwards we used the room to sleep in, sharing the same bed. It was common that adult men slept next to each other without anyone assuming anything might be going on. For one thing sharing a bed was a sign of friendship, and that evening we had become close friends, and I felt drawn to him. At first I wasn't sure about the strong desires I felt towards him. I was thinking of the fear of getting caught, the curiosity and confusion, the threat of exposure, the furtive glances. But from the moment I looked at the shine in his eyes, I knew. There was a current, a note of understanding, and our desire erupted like a volcano. I had to make a decision. I had to work out whether our roots had so entwined together that it was beyond belief if I should ever part.

In the middle of the night, I was woken by heavy

footsteps climbing the wooden stairs. I opened my eyes, but I couldn't see anything, the room was pitch-dark. I felt Deryk lying next to me, his arms holding my body, and I heard a group of men entering the landing. Someone was pushing against the door, breaking the lock, and the door was pushed open. Instantly I looked up and saw a man storming in, holding a lantern, illuminating the dark room. His eyes were fixed on me as he walked to the bed, and pulled away the woollen bed spread. Deryk and I lay there, revealing our bodies fully naked. The Sheriff, quickly followed by his men, could tell from our closeness that we had become more than friends and the expression on his face showed his disapproval.

"They say do not revile the king even in your thoughts, or curse the rich in your bedroom, because a bird in the sky may carry your words, and a bird on the wing may report what you say. Tonight a little bird came to me, and revealed to me you've committed many sins in this house and its cellars, reading from the Luther Bible, holding a service in English, and having entered this room, I've even encountered another sin, the act of sodomy. The Queen will soon find out what happened in this doomed place, but first, I will bring you to Her Royal Highness's Council. You will be begging them for forgiveness!"

"Listen, friend, whoever your little bird is, and whatever he or she told you, I can do whatever I want behind

closed doors." Deryk retaliated. "I refuse to visit the priest and neither shall I confess or ask for forgiveness. Should I wish to, I can do that in my own home."
The Sheriff ignored him and, picking up the Luther Bible, looked down at us.
'Deryk Carver and John Launder, you're both under arrest for praying and reading from this book which has been banned. But, I will also notify the Bishop of anything that I have witnessed in this dwelling, and I wash my hands of any guilt should he consider sentencing you for sodomy too. Get dressed and get ready for a preliminary meeting with the Queen's Council.'
"It's so sad to hear your story," said Rick, "and I'm really sorry to hear you had to go through all this. These days, most unjust laws have been overturned in this country: people are no longer put into prison because of their faith and people are treated equally regardless of their sexuality." Rick sat on the floor looking down at the hat in his hands. "I guess there were good times and bad times during the century you lived in - it's pretty much like today, and although we have human rights and laws, there's still so much to be learned. Now, tell me, what happened after you attended the meeting?"
'Well, after the ad-hoc meeting, the Queen's Council decided we would be sent to Newgate Prison in London. It's almost impossible to describe what I saw when I was

first brought in. I looked around upon all the horrors of that dismal place, home to nearly three hundred prisoners. They were kept herded into tiny cells behind rusted iron bars, with some prisoners left chained to the wall to languish and starve. There was a lack of air and water, and the stench was unbearable. The place seemed an emblem of hell itself, like a kind of entrance to it. Upon arrival we were chained, and led to the dirty, stinking and dark unlit dungeons, where we were treated cruelly by the guards. They inflicted punishment on prisoners before their sentences even began. It didn't matter what the criminal had done or whether they were awaiting trial, everyone was treated the same way, unless you had money. Fortunately, Deryk had plenty of it. He could afford a cell in one of the better wards, and after the first payment was made, both of us were moved to the new cell. Every month Deryk's staff would travel to Newgate Prison, handing over a bag of money to the keeper to ensure we could continue to reside in the same cell. They would provide us with food, beer and beds, because one who could not afford a bed would sleep on a coverlet with dirty straw. They kept us there for months, nine in total, making more money each time our trial was delayed - but believe me, time was more valuable than money. I loved him like my own soul: we ate at the same table and shared the same dish.

'I found myself in unfamiliar territory when I, the

unquestionably married man, realised I had fallen in love with my best friend, with a man who was married too. A man I had only met twice. A man I had never before even thought of in a romantic way.

'It all came down to this moment, one moment when he was rinsing the cutlery and plates in a wooden pail of cold water, and he looked over and smiled at me. I knew this was it. This was the moment when I had to decide if I could allow myself to love a man against everything I had previously known about myself. This was the moment when I had to decide if I was going to take a step forward into this crazy idea of telling my best friend that I loved him, despite the fact we had no hope and no future. So I approached him, cautiously, I could hear my heart beating in my ears. I opened my mouth and no words came out. Again, I tried, and all I could say was, "Deryk, I have something to tell you."

He looked at me earnestly.

"Deryk, I think I'm in love with you."

His expression changed to that of confusion.

"Well, you've been so great and taken care of me, and I know it doesn't make much sense. But, if I've ever felt love, this is it. And, well, I think I'm in love with you."

He stopped and thought for a moment. It was a long moment. Then he opened his mouth again and asked, "Did you miss me after the first time we met?"

I nodded my head slowly, uneasily.

"Were you excited to see me again?"
I nodded again, this time with a hint of uncertainty.
He looked back timidly. "Well, then I think I might love you too."

'Our love was like a flame, burning bright inside this living hell, and that was all that mattered.
Every day, the prison wardens allowed us to go outside for an hour to get some fresh air, where we met other inmates who asked us quite frankly why we were put into prison. It turned out heresy was the most common reason, along with smugglers and murderers. Through the inmates, we found out that laws against sodomy, or buggery as we called it, did not come into existence in England until the 1530s, coinciding with Henry VIII's break with Rome. At this time, a law was passed making sodomy an offence and therefore potentially punishable by execution, varying according to the social standing of the condemned. This, of course, left me very worried, as the Sheriff had accused us of heresy and sodomy. Deryk suspected that the royal attitude towards sodomy was probably consistent with that of the majority of the population, officially condemned when it resulted in public scandal, but often tolerated if kept private, especially if the person was wealthy and had social status. Some kings and queens were rumoured to have had numerous same-sex lovers, during perhaps the most

homophobic era of human history. By the time we had spoken to other inmates, we found out that, after Queen Mary had ascended the English throne, all of the laws that had been passed by Henry VIII had been revoked, so at least we could not be executed for sodomy. But, after several months of being kept in prison, the investigation found both Deryk and me guilty of heresy.

'Over the period leading up to our conviction, we made many confessions which were recorded in writing, signed by both of us, sealing our fate as a heretic in the eyes of the Catholic Church. We always stood by our word that we would not recant.

'One month later on 10th June 1555, we were taken to the Consistory Court situated in the Saint Paul's Cathedral, the longest church in the world with one of the tallest spires I had ever seen. The Sheriff took us to the entrance gate, our handcuffs clinking as we crossed the church square. We passed crowds of people gathered around St Paul's Cross, a pulpit standing in the open air, which was not only attended by religious people, but also used as a public space for executions like burning people at the stake.

'After we entered the church we were brought unto the Bishop of London, Edmund Bonner, and his consistory. The people called him "Bloody Bonner", a terrible man appointed by Queen Mary to deal with religious

dissidents, and he was just what she needed as he started persecuting the Protestants, stamping out religious dissent, with all his devotion. Bonner had no pity or compassion for the people brought before him. We soon found out the truth of the rumour that he would call for rods to beat stubborn witnesses.

'We were taken into the court room, a heavy-oak furnished enclosure with benches surrounding a large table where Bonner was seated in a high chair on the dais, looking at us with disgust. With a cold stare he took the documents detailing the accusations made against us, and I could tell that he really gave no quarter.

"Today, you've appeared to myself and the consistory because you've been accused of heresy. Last year the Heresy Act was revived and an order was issued that everyone should go to their priest for confession and attending Mass. The same order also obliged people to report everyone who has been seen reading the Luther Bible including the Book of the Gospels, and who opposed the veneration of relics and the communion of saints to the Sheriff.

'You both admitted that, during the Queen's reign, you had read the bible on many occasions at your house and brewery in Brighthelmstone, and you knew it had been banned by Queen Mary.

'You carried on with your unacceptable behaviour, and as a result, you've become victims of your own stupidity. The

Queen's law was made public in every single church and pub by your local town criers on the streets, and distributed in weekly written announcements. Both of you confessed you were aware of the changes in law, as you have confirmed previously, and in the end you only have yourself to blame. I have tried to persuade you to recant, but you wouldn't listen, I've beaten you with a rod but you wouldn't budge, instead you kept on clinging on to your own belief. Our priests even suggested to you to purchase a Letter of Indulgence to absolve all your sins so the law would not reach you, but again you refused.
'You have been incredibly difficult to deal with, but I'm going to offer you the final opportunity to tell us whether you agree with these written confessions signed by both of you, or not. If you disagree, you'll be able to recant and return to Roman Catholicism, and if you do so, you'll be able to walk out as free men. If you agree with everything you've said, and decide not to recant, you will face your final punishment. It's up to you now, and I honestly don't care what you decide."
'The Bishop turned to Deryk: "To start with you, Deryk Carver, would you consider recanting?"
' "Over my dead body! I agree with every single statement I've made," he said with a fierce and proud look. "If you can make a man out of bread and wine, then you can surely make me a pudding out of it as well?" he said to prove his point. "If Christ were here you would

sentence him to a worse death than he was put to before!"
The bishop ignored him, turned to me and said: "John Launder, would you consider recanting?"
' "I will never stray from these answers so long as I live! I'd rather go to hell instead of living a lie." I stared at him with an intense and fearless look.
' "Today both of you have stated you firmly stick to your beliefs, and after we wasted eight months of our time on your trial, the Consistory and I will accept your decision. Hereby, I, the Bishop of London, declare Deryk Carver and John Launder, in the name of Queen Mary, to be sentenced for the act of heresy which was committed in The Black Lion brewery in Brighthelmstone on All Hallows' Eve 31st October 1554.
' "Deryk Carver and John Lauder, you leave us no other choice than to deliver you back to the Sheriff Edward Cage. Today, he will be taking both of you to Lewes, and I condemn you to be burned at the stake for your unforgivable sins and may God have mercy upon your souls and by suffering purify your souls until you find the love of God."

'The Bishop and Consistory vacated their seats and walked away. The Sheriff took us back to the entrance gate, where a horse and cart was waiting to bring us to the cellars of the Star Inn. The same cellars where we are standing now.

'The following month, Deryk was the first martyr to be burned. He was proud to die for what he believed in, and so was I, paying the same price the following day in Steyning, a town I'd never ever visited before.'
Rick looked at him with sorrowful eyes. "I can feel your pain - you and Deryk were secret lovers. You intended to spend the rest of your lives together, until your lives were brutally torn apart, and I empathise with you. Even after all these years, I can sense you're longing to see him and hold him, but instead your souls have drifted apart."
'Ever since the day he died, my soul travels between Lewes and Steyning, the sites we were burned, over and over again, and I can't seem to find him. There isn't much time left.'
"After everything you've told me, I'm obliged to help you to find the love of your life. Please tell me how I can bring him back to you."
'Thank you, I really appreciate your help. You need to find someone who has a strong connection with Deryk. It could be a relative, or someone who owns his brewery and inn, if there's anything left of it?'
"The brewery and inn have been demolished, but they've rebuilt his house and it's now called The Black Lion. But, I'm staying in one of the old cottages around the corner, and they're still in the original state, dating back to the sixteenth century.

It's owned by a guy named Matt."
'Rick, you're a godsend! The cottages were built by Deryk, he put his heart and soul into it. Here, take his hat and give it to Matt. It will help him to find Deryk, and when he does, tell him to speak my name. It's the only thing I'm asking for.'
John ascended the steps, had a quick glance back at Rick and saluted him before he rose up into the air through the hole, gliding over the wings of the angels who were sitting at the bottom of the War Memorial, vanishing into the dark sky.

People had gathered around Rick as he lay on the cracked glass panel above the steps leading to the cellar. They looked worried at his collapse. As he regained consciousness, Rick heard people whispering, and his head hurt. He opened his eyes, looked up at the winged angels of the memorial towering high above him, and touched his head.
"What on earth has happened to me? Just a minute ago I fell through the panel."
"Are you ok? We were all very worried after you suddenly collapsed. Instead of falling through the panel, you fell on it." The tour guide looked noticeably concerned whilst he was shining his lantern at him. "Do you need a Doctor?"
"My head hurts a little bit, but I'm sure I'll be fine."

"Is there anything I can do for you?"
"Erm, actually yes, there is something you could do. If you don't mind, could you order me a taxi, please?"
"Of course, I'll get you a taxi. It's the least I can do. Oh, before I forget, I found this next to you on the street, if I'm not mistaken I think it belongs to you." The man swiftly handed him the black medieval hat.

The taxi driver dropped Rick off outside the Cricketers. He entered the pub, ordered a drink, and sat down on the plush red velvet seating looking at the old photographs and framed prints lining the walls and the ceiling when a man approached him.
"Do you mind if I sit here?" He asked, pointing at the empty seat next to him.
"Yes, that's fine."
"Thanks. I love the hat on the table, is it yours?"
"Well, not exactly. I went to Lewes to attend a ghost walk, until something strange occurred outside the Town Hall."
"What happened?"
Perhaps it was the blow to his head or perhaps it was the alcohol, but Rick found himself inclined to trust the stranger. He laughed a little ruefully, as if he expected not to be believed, and said, "I remember I fell through the glass panel and found

an old medieval black hat at the bottom of the steps."

"Are you ok?"

"Yes, I'm ok, my head hurts a little, that's all. You probably won't believe me, but I encountered a man in the vaults below the Town Hall, a spirit, who has been guarding the undercroft for centuries, and he told me his sorrowful story. But, it's getting more weird. After that, he ascended through the same hole I fell through, and disappeared into the sky. The next moment I regained consciousness outside the town hall near the war memorial, and the tour guide told me I had fainted and hit my head on the pavement. After he phoned a taxi to take me back to Brighton, he handed me the same hat which I had found in the cellars. Nobody was able to explain where it came from."

The stranger, who had listened intently, paused to digest the story; then he said thoughtfully,

"Glad to hear you're ok, but it all sounds very mysterious. They say, there is life after death, and sometimes these two worlds meet."

"Those are the exact words the tour-guide spoke!"

"I still remember his wise words after I attended the same walk a couple of years ago. I'm intrigued about your encounter with the spirit. Did it feel real to you?"

"Yes, it did. First of all he was surprised I could see him. I touched his cold hands, and I listened to his life-story, and I believed every single word he said, it was so intense. Do spirits intrigue you then?"
"Yes, they do, but I'm also intrigued by people who can see and feel spirits. The way you described it, I think you're telling the truth."
"I really appreciate that." Rick felt he could trust this man and opened up to him about the encounter with the spirit, telling him the whole story of Deryk and John.
"Nowadays John is trapped in a world of spirits between Lewes and Steyning. He believes that Deryk's spirit is still wandering the streets, day and night, but he doesn't know where he is, and his only hope is that Deryk will find him."
"Their spirits have been separated since death, and I hope John will find Deryk, to reconcile."
"So do I. He said he was looking to find someone who has a connection with Deryk, someone who was a relative, or owns his land. I explained to him there was not much left of his brewery and inn, except for the rebuilt pub and a small row of sixteenth century cottages behind it where I'm staying. John said they were built by Deryk and he begged me to find the owner of the cottages. I told him I've never met the owner as I made the booking on the

internet, but I promised to do my best to find him."
"Well, I guess you're lucky. You may not realise it, but you've found him. He's sitting right here in front of you. I am the owner of the Black Lion Cottage."
"What? Are you Matt? What a coincidence!"
It was the first time the men met in real life and politely they shook each others' hands.
"How nice to meet you, Matt, I guess it was meant to be."
"It's nice to meet you too, Rick, it was destined to happen. Spirits are often messengers and appear to us when something needs to be done. Do you happen to remember if he requested anything specifically?"
"Yes, he did. John said to give Deryk's hat to you when I should meet you." Rick picked it up from the table and gave it to Matt. "It will help you to find Deryk, and when you do, tell him to speak John's name. That's what John asked me."
"I know of Deryk's pub, his cottage, and the ongoing stories about him haunting the old town, but so far, I have not encountered his spirit."
"Well, you'll never know! John believes you may be the 'chosen one'. Can I ask you a question?"
"Yes, sure."
"Did you happen to have any encounters with spirits before?"

"I am receptive to spirits, and yes, I have encountered them, just like you did today. My first happened one evening after a show in the bar of the Old Vic theatre in Bristol - I was visiting some friends - it was quite frightening and I still remember the day like it was yesterday. Everyone had left the theatre and I walked to the bar where I ordered a drink. I could smell a whiff of lavender perfume, but this was weird as I was the only person in the bar. Then I heard her voice, and even felt her breath on my face. I could see a lady standing in front of me, dressed in a black velvet dress, looking like a celebrity. In my head I could hear her voice and she said to me. *'I'm Sarah Siddons, the widow of the theatre manager, I cannot bear to leave this place I loved most in life.'*
"She moved towards me, smiled, and in an instant her spirit stepped through my body. I can still hear her giggling whilst I'm telling you this story. It was a spine-chilling experience."
"I bet it was and it's even scared me. Look, I've got goose bumps all over my arms." Rick looked at his watch: it was nearly eleven. "I'm really sorry, Matt, but I feel very tired and my brain is tired too, it's been a long day."

"I understand, and should I encounter Deryk's spirit, I promise I will speak John's name, and tell him where to find him."
"Thank you, I'm sure John will be very grateful. It was lovely to meet you - let's keep in touch."
"It was really good to meet you too, Rick, we've got a connection. Let's catch up again sometime soon."

Booking Cancellation

A few weeks later, Matt was looking at the stunning sea views from the balcony of his penthouse when his phone pinged. It displayed an email from Pete and Sam. Due to a slight change of plans they'd cancelled their booking at Black Lion Cottage, and instead they would be staying at a cottage in Steyning. Their change of location prompted a curiosity in Matt. It immediately brought to mind what Rick had told him about John's ghost trapped in a world of spirits between Lewes and Steyning. The curious meeting in The Cricketers was still buzzing in his head so he looked on the internet to find out more about the history of the town, discovering many interesting facts. Steyning had a fine high street, plenty of old buildings including Tudor style half timbered houses, and residents had some lovely countryside on their doorstep. It certainly looked like a fascinating place to stay, with lots of connections to medieval times.

Afterwards, he used the rest of the afternoon to do a full audit of his cottage, starting at the top floor and working his way down the narrow stairs to the living room. Pleased to see that the beds, wardrobes and curtains were still in pretty good shape, he decided that he could do with a drink and checked the time. It was just after five: "wine o'clock" then.

He was about to lock the front door when he saw a man all dressed in black entering the narrow lane; and from the moment their eyes met, Matt felt impelled to hold the man's gaze. It was like the rest of the world faded to grey while their souls were momentarily connected in the mutual knowledge that they were looking at each other without blinking an eye. Somebody tapped him on the shoulder and he turned around.
"Excuse me?"
It was a woman, a brunette, dressed in a beautiful light pink cotton jacket and a matching pair of trousers. She had entered the narrow lane from the opposite direction and, unintentionally, he prevented her from getting past him.
"Oh, I'm sorry, am I standing in your way?" He stepped back to let the lady pass and his eyes followed her, but when he looked round, the man who had entered the lane earlier was nowhere to be seen. Matt knew this lane very well: if the man had decided to turn around, he would still be within his vicinity, but instead he had inexplicably

disappeared. The conversation with Rick sprung to his mind again and he remembered the promise he had made. He had said he would speak John's name should he ever encounter Deryk's spirit, and he had promised to give him the hat as a sign from John (he kept it with him always, the old soft material rolled up in his inside pocket) but as he thought this, he realised, he didn't know what he looked like. How would he recognise him? He wondered how this spirit would appear - would it be a semi-transparent figure, a kind of energy floating in the air? Or would it feel real and solid? He speculated that perhaps the way it appeared to him would have something to do with his own receptiveness to the spirit plane. Matt, not knowing the answer to this pivotal question, turned right into Black Lion Street, entered the pub where he ordered a glass of red, and sat down in the far corner of the pub to enjoy it.

In front of him stood a display of two skeletons propped in a chair, one wearing a black top hat, the other had a black and white bow-tie pinned on its skull. They were seated in front of a table decorated with a large black candelabra holding dripping candles, china plates printed with skeleton bones, and miniature pumpkins carved into crude faces with candles placed in it, like impromptu lanterns.

He had forgotten it was Hallowe'en, the last day of October, known as All Hallows' Eve. It used to be a religious evening, when bells rang out at sunset for departed souls, people lit candles on gravestones and left them burning all night in the darkness and solitude of the cemetery, whilst ghosts were haunting empty churches.

The barmaid smiled at Matt as she was putting some candles on the table to try and create atmosphere.

"Hi Matt, how lovely to see you. I don't see you hanging around here very often. What brought you to the pub today?"

"It's lovely to see you too, Liz. My guests cancelled their booking - it was a last minute cancellation, so I decided to spend my time wisely and did an audit before I decided to have a drink. What have you been up to?"

"Getting the pub ready for tonight. It's going to be a busy one, Saturday night and Hallowe'en night."

As she went to place more candles on another table, she heard footsteps going across the wooden floor. She clearly felt the vibration through the floorboards. Suddenly a candle was pushed off the table, and fell down right in front of her.

"I think Deryk is back! His spirit has become quite agitated over the last couple of weeks." She caught Matt's eyes. "I've grown used to it. Lights going on

and off, I've heard whispering coming from the cellar. Last week after I had unpacked some boxes and was about to leave the room, the door slammed shut right in front of my face, with such force it rattled in its frame. But today, it feels different - I've never seen a candle being pushed off the table before."
"I have been told about Deryk's spirit," said Matt thoughtfully, finding it odd that his inner questions were so quickly echoed, "and it sounds like he's restless. Do you have any idea why he's so agitated?"
"Well, all I can think of is that it has to do with the anniversary of the day he was arrested and sent to prison. They say that he never set foot in The Black Lion again. I guess he has enough reasons to feel frustrated."
"Mmm, I guess so, but there's clearly something not right and I wonder what he is up to."
Liz raised an eyebrow at this remark but he did not notice.
Matt drained his glass of wine as a group of young men walked into the bar, all of them in their mid- to early twenties.
"Hi, can I have four lagers please?" one of the men asked.
"Do you want the usual or the special?" said the bartender

"What's the special?"
"A bottle of blond Belgian beer with a hint of lemon."
"I'll have four of those then, please."
"Good choice. Just give me a minute whilst I fetch them for you."
Before he dived down behind the bar to retrieve them from the fridge, he caught Matt's eye and spotted an empty glass. "I'll be with you in a minute, sir." Straightening up, he handed the bottles over.
"Here you go, four blond Belgian beers,"
"Thank you," the man said.
Making conversation, the bartender asked him if there was a slight accent to his voice.
"Well spotted, I'm from Belgium. The name's Pascal."
"Ah, I'm from Belgium too! I was born in Liège."
"So was I! What a coincidence. How did you end up here?"
"It's a long story, mate. A very long story. But it's great that you and your pals have come all the way down here." Opening the first bottle of beer, the bartender poured it into a glass. "These are on me," he said as he handed it over to Pascal.
Whilst this exchange was going on, Matt was gazing almost absentmindedly at the unlit candle in front of him, put there by the barmaid. It was a new

candle, but it looked old. Reaching out, he let his finger run from the edge to the wick, still as perfectly smooth as the day it was made, ready to fulfil its purpose. Sniffing at his finger, he inhaled the the sweet smell of beeswax. Having a lighter on him, he retrieved it and, hoping the bartender wouldn't mind, lit the candle, watching the new flame flicker bright, golden light. This was better, this did indeed create a cosy atmosphere. He settled back in his chair, feeling content, happy with life. The candle light was still busy flickering when his eyes landed on a pile of ancient envelopes and letters with broken seals on the chair next to him. Why would someone leave a pile of letters like these on a chair? Intrigued, he couldn't resist picking up one of the letters, and to his surprise, it was addressed to Deryk Carver, the very same man that Rick had been so insistent that he try to contact, whose ghost the barmaid had just been discussing; and thinking back, he remembered that his friend Kate had told him about Deryk at the leaving do before he had even bought Black Lion Cottage. This must be more than a coincidence. The letter was dated 1554.
He was more than surprised, he was awe-struck. Somebody had written these letters to a man who had died over four hundred years ago, when most

people were illiterate. Were they delivered by a travelling merchant, or perhaps a pilgrim passing from one town to another, or a mutual friend? These letters should be in a museum, not left here, on a chair in this pub, forgotten about! A strange feeling came over him: he felt compelled to read them, getting to know their secrets. He felt that it would pull him further into this mystery from so long ago - and he wasn't sure that he could spare the mental and emotional energy. He looked around him and noticed no one was paying attention to him. Curiosity dominated his common sense, and casually he picked up the letter from the top, and put it in front him.

Dear Deryk,

I have received a letter from you written the seventeenth day of September, at Brighthelmstone, the which letter I have well understood and all things therein contained whereof thank you and for your good and true heart. It has been a pleasure to meet you at Mid Summer, and before the month of the Blood Moon I shall ride to the sea with the company of my comrade Thomas Iveson to listen to the gospel God had forbid. I pray you to accept this bill for my messenger to recommend me to you in my most faithful wise, as he that fainest of all other desires to know of your welfare, which I pray God increase to your most pleasure. Yet when you have read this letter I pray you burn it or keep it secret to yourself, as my faithful trust is in you. I am your man and ever will be, by the grace of God, which ever have you in his keeping. Farewell most heartily; and love me, as I love you, and think upon me, as I thinketh upon you.

Yours

J

This was a passionate letter written in old-fashioned English, intriguingly by a man declaring his love for another man in a time when intimacy between two men or two women was considered to be sinful. He begged him to keep the infidelity secret.
From whom? Perhaps from his wife? And what about "J", an initial he presumed to be short for John, did he also have a wife? If so, "J" was in the same boat, not willing to jeopardise his marriage; and another man in the same position would understand that. Unable to judge the situation, the affair must have been a burden for Deryk which caused him to divert his love from his wife.
According to the letter John had written, she was unaware of anything, but she must have suffered too

and had the right to know what was going on. Matt wondered whether she ever found out?
The flame of the candle on the table flickered, reacting to a sudden movement of air, and he felt a presence, like somebody standing close to him. Quickly he puts the letter back on the chair. He looked up and in front of the table stood a bearded man, wearing a black coat and leather boots, holding a bottle of wine.
"Oh, sorry, was this your table?" Matt asked.
"Don't worry, there's always room for a handsome man like you," he said with a flirtatious smile. The man pulled a chair and sat down opposite Matt. Matt stared at him, confused about what he had said. His eyes looked familiar, and he was sure he had seen them before, but where?
"I can tell from the residue in your glass you were drinking red wine. Fancy sharing this bottle of red with me to celebrate Hallowe'en?"
"If you're paying, that's fine." Matt said with a smile. The man poured the wine into two tumblers and sat himself down opposite Matt.
"Bottoms up!" Their tumblers clinked and they took a sip of wine.
"You may or may not believe in ghosts, but this Hallowe'en along with the screeching herring gulls in the pale moonlight, you may want to take a few

minutes to appreciate the role of ghosts in our haunted pasts, and how they guide us to lead our lives. Now, tell me young man, what do you know about Hallowe'en?"

"Well, I know people scoop out the flesh of pumpkins, carve faces in them, place candles in it and put them outside. When it gets dark, children dress up and go to people's houses, knocking on their door for treats, and as the door is opened they yell 'Trick or Treat' holding out their bags. Those who will not give out a treat have to be careful as they may be tricked with a joke instead, or risk getting their pumpkin smashed!"

The man laughed. "I like your sense of humour, but the story I remember is more gruesome than you think. Pumpkins with ghoulish faces, illuminated by candles; they're a sign of the modern Hallowe'en season. But the practice of decorating Jack O' Lanterns originated in Ireland, where large turnips were used as lanterns."

"I knew it originated in Ireland but I always wondered why they were called 'Jack O'Lanterns'."

"The name comes from an Irish myth about a vile person named Jack, nicknamed Stingy Jack, who travelled the country deceiving and manipulating people. According to the story, one evening Stingy Jack came upon a body with an eerie grimace on his face, it turned out to be Satan, and he feared he had appeared to him to collect his soul. Jack made a last request and begged him to let him have a drink in the local pub, and Satan, patiently waiting to take his soul, supplied him with plenty of drinks. After he had quenched his thirst, he asked the Devil to turn himself into a silver coin in order to pay the bill. Satan, impressed by Jack's clever tactic, did metamorphose, but Jack decided to keep the silver coin and put it into his pocket next to a silver crucifix, preventing the Devil from changing back into his original form. Eventually Jack freed the Devil, under the condition that he would not claim his soul for ten years.

Ten years later, the day had come the Devil would claim Jack's soul, but Jack had a final request and asked if he could have an apple as he didn't want to die with an empty stomach. Whilst the Devil climbed into the tree to pick a piece of fruit, Jack carved a sign of a crucifix into the tree's bark so that the Devil could not come down until the Devil promised Jack not to claim his soul for another decade.

'Eventually, drinking took its toll on Jack and two years later, after his last encounter with the Devil, he died. His soul prepared itself to enter Heaven, but he was abruptly stopped. Jack was told by God that because of his sinful lifestyle, he was not allowed into Heaven. Jack made his way down the bowls of the Earth and arrived at the Gates of Hell where he begged for admission into the underworld. Satan, hadn't forgotten about the tricks Jack played on him and had promised not to claim his soul, gave Jack an ember and sent him off into the dark night letting him suffer in eternity. Jack put the coal into a carved-out turnip and has been roaming the cold earth ever since. Irish families who emigrated to America, whose ancestors referred to this ghostly figure as 'Jack of the Lantern' abbreviated it to 'Jack O'Lantern' and adopted the tradition of doing the same with pumpkins to help guide spirits."

"So the carved pumpkin has a spooky story of its own, starring the Devil himself. How apt is that!" said Matt.

"Not many people know the real story, and over time the pagan celebration Samhain, an ancient Celtic festival, became All Hallows' Eve, and is now the root of Hallowe'en."

"That's fascinating. Samhain was the division of the year between Summer and Winter," said Matt, "and spookily enough, when the division between this world and the Otherworld was at its thinnest, allowing spirits to pass through. We know this phenomenon is still strongly connected to

Hallowe'en, but what about all the dressing up, did the Irish emigrants in America invent that?"
"During my lifetime, children would dress up in costumes carrying turnip lanterns lit with burning coal, and perform actual tricks in exchange for flowers. At the time, many people believed that the spirits of those who had passed, no matter how good or bad, would come back to haunt the living on the night of All Hallows' Eve. They even believed by wearing masks and disguises, the dead spirits would be unable to harm them and continued to ward them off with candles, lanterns, and bonfires. Not only did the pagans believe that spirits of the dead continued to exist, the belief also became part of many early church practices."
For a moment Matt wondered whether this man could be telling the truth. The man knew a lot about the origins of Hallowe'en and he had explained it in very precise detail. Details he had never heard of before.
"That's interesting. Even nowadays we use candles, lanterns, and bonfires to ward off ghosts, like they do in Lewes, also known as the capital of bonfires. I believe the earliest known bonfire night took place in a street of Lewes near the old Star Inn, which is now the Town Hall. Every year the town celebrates the foiling of the plot to blow up Parliament in 1605

but it also commemorates the Lewes Martyrs on the 5th November, just a week after Hallowe'en."
The man grabbed the bottle and poured another glass. "After all these years, I'm grateful to know, the people of Lewes still commemorate the martyrs, who were imprisoned in the vaults below the old Star Inn, before they were burned. But, somehow, I need to explain that Hallowe'en, or All Hallows' Eve, is not only about warding off spirits and commemorating them, it's about spirits of the dead which continue to exist. Between you and me, try to imagine you live in a time where people were publicly executed in the centre of town squares like a market or a green, surrounded by crowds who witnessed people being hanged, quartered, and burned.'
Matt was quiet. He looked the man in the eye, trying to process what he just said.
"At the time the Catholic Church strongly believed that if the soul was not bad enough to be sent to an eternity of damnation in hell, and not good enough to go to heaven either, it was in an intermediate state after physical death, known as purgatory. It's a place where spirits of a dead person are sent to suffer for their sins, and to be purified before they go to heaven."
The man put down his glass. "I'm sorry if I've been

bothering you with my talks about past times. It's all I can remember from when I was a living soul, many centuries ago, and I wanted to share it with someone like you. In all those centuries of living in solitude and not being being able to communicate with anyone, you're the first person who can see me and hear me talking."

At these words, Matt felt as if something he had known in his heart all through their conversation, but had not been able to name in his head, had been confirmed. He was talking and drinking with a spirit - but would an independent witness be able to see what he himself was seeing? Was the conversation taking place aloud or in his mind?

"My name is Deryk Carver and, as you probably know, I died many centuries ago."

Matt gave him a nod and gestured with his hand to continue his story.

"Before my death, Bishop Bonner suggested that if I paid for a slip of paper, called an Indulgence, it would allow my spirit to escape Purgatory. People were deceived by paying money to the Church, so I politely declined.

"At first, as a Protestant myself, I didn't believe in a place where the souls of those have died in a fire would undergo a further amount of suffering to expiate their sins of moral sin, until something happened to me after I was burned at the stake in Lewes.

"Due to the intense heat of the fire, my spirit felt there was something seriously wrong and released itself with great force from my body. Separated for the first time and engulfed in flames, my spirit panicked and rose with the smoke and the ashes, finding its way to the black and golden gateway to heaven, hidden high in the sky. Just like Stingy Jack I was in a state between death and something else, something I was unable to describe, but I knew my spirit was deeply connected with the scenes of nature: it felt the soft wind, it could see the bright light, and it felt the sultry summer temperature in the sky. Coming from behind the clouds I heard a voice, and I can still remember the exact words the man spoke.

" 'You are denied entrance. Your soul should be damned, just as your body has been burned, but I will lay a last commandment upon you: to return and live amongst the undead until, perhaps, one day, you can find the soul of the friend you had to leave behind. And then your souls will rise together and return to these gates, and I will reconsider. You are denied entrance, for now.'

"Saint Peter had prevented me from entering heaven, and instead, I would be living as a spirit, together with other doomed and lonely spirits in agony unless I could find my friend.

"After a long time of crossing many roads and many hills, my spirit was relieved to find its way back to The Black Lion, but I had been undead for centuries and came to the conclusion this state of purification had become a torment. I wished things were like they were back in the old days, when I was working in the brewery and inn.

Back then, both me and my wife were brewers, but she also managed to look after the cottages which we offered to our guests to stay. She made the beds, cooked breakfast, and she was looking after our children. My wife would always warn me when there was any danger so I could hide in the pantry. She was aware and allowed me to meet men and engage with them, but it turned out she was not happy about the situation.

'One stormy night, when Sheriff Cage and his men climbed the stairs and found me and my friend John in the upstairs room, she had not come up to warn me. It has always nagged at me as to why she didn't. I just couldn't put my finger on it, until later when she came to visit me at Newgate Prison. We met in the communal square, she was accompanied by Cage, and to my surprise they were holding each other's hands, I couldn't believe what I saw. She looked at me with disgust and I gathered this was going to be a short and unpleasant visit. She kept her distance. 'We both know why you're here. You were arrested for heresy, but do you know who turned you in? Well, I guess you don't! A week before you were arrested, you received a letter from John whilst you were working in the brewery. I hastened to see Cage and showed him the letter to prove you were going to read from the forbidden book. The day came and all the men arrived to listen to the words of your forbidden book. Later that evening, when you and John went upstairs, I ran to Cage's office to tell him what had happened. I had chosen not to warn you, as for many years I've witnessed your sins, and I simply couldn't bear it any longer. Was I recruited to brew beer, look after the cottages, brewery and inn, whilst you could read out loud from the forbidden book and fool around with whoever you fancied? Let me remind you, I'm a Catholic, and I betrayed you and John, for better or worse. This is the last you will see of me. You're a heretic! May your soul burn in hell!'"

Matt, not saying a word, stared at him, taking in everything the man had said, and knocked back his wine.

"You're a great listener and I beg you, have one more drink with me, and I'll tell you the rest of my

story." The man refilled their tumblers.
"Thank you. I'd love to have another drink with you, but I guess I already know the rest of your story, Deryk." He looked the man straight into his eyes; it was then he recognised his powerful gaze. It was of the same man he encountered in the narrow lane around the corner, before he inexplicably disappeared.
"You're the owner of The Black Lion, founded back in the sixteenth century. You have risen from the ashes, revived from its funeral pyre with renewed youth to haunt the living, just like Jack O' Lantern did, trying to find his way in the Otherworld, the destination of the spirits of the dead."
"My spirit feels tired of haunting the living, depleted, I no longer feel passionate about anything," said Deryk wearily. "My spirit is trapped in the Otherworld. What can I do, where can I go?" In one gulp, Deryk drained his tumbler and put it back on the table.
"You're not the only one who is trapped in the Otherworld and there's something I need to tell you. Someone has been looking for you and his spirit is roaming the dark shadows across the hills. Ironically, you've mentioned his name before, his name is John." Matt watched the bewildered look on Deryk's face.

"John? Looking for me? I can't believe it! The last time I saw him was when he was standing outside the Star Inn where they tortured me, and he fell to his knees in tears, but he was still alive. I remember we were both sentenced to death, to burn in eternity. They decided to end our lives on different days, in different places. I dare not imagine the horrible things that must have happened to him, his destiny must have been as cruel and painful as mine." Deryk looked at Matt begging for an explanation. "I have a feeling you know what might have happened to John. Do you know where I can find his spirit?"
"I haven't encountered John's spirit personally, but yesterday I spoke to a guy called Rick and he told me he had met John in the cellars below a building known to you as the Star Inn. He shared John's entire story with me. And he gave me this - I believe it's yours!" Matt took out the old hat and laid it on the table.
Deryk's eyes widened. "My hat! And the Star Inn - it's where John and I were kept imprisoned. Did he say where his soul travels?"
"Yes, he did, he told Rick his soul travels between Lewes and Steyning, every day and night."
Deryk frowned . "I cannot return to Lewes. The memories of death keep me away from that town.

The Sheriff told us we would be burned in places we had no connection with, to spread fear amongst other people. I vaguely seem to remember the name Steyning, a town somewhere near a port and Bramber castle, north of the South Downs. I've never been there."

With sudden realisation dawning in his eyes, Deryk looked at Matt. "His spirit must be wandering around in Steyning."

Matt stood up: "You could well be right. Why don't you go there to find out? You've got nothing to lose."

"But, how do I get there?" asked Deryk.

"I'll phone us a taxi, I'll get you to him."

Within ten minutes, a taxi arrived and stopped outside the pub. The driver opened his window.

"Where to?"

"To Steyning, please."

Matt got into the taxi, accompanied by Deryk. He wondered if the driver was able to see his spirit passenger or not. He looked thoughtfully out of the window. They were heading towards Steyning.

Deryk

The taxi drove from Brighton to the Shoreham Bypass with the backdrop of the iconic gothic structure Lancing College Chapel, overlooking the River Adur, loomed in the distance as we followed the road adjacent to the river leading to the picturesque town of Steyning.
We turned into Church Street, a country lane with tall trees towering over timber cottages, and I had an inexplicable feeling this was the place where I might find John. Matt asked the driver to stop and we both got out of the taxi, and faced the front of a beautiful two storey, red-brick property called Chantry Green House. It had five windows and two dormers overlooking an idyllic garden. The air was filled with the smell of sweet flowers, woody trees and musky moss, and behind it was a babbling brook with an old track going down through the trees leading to the local church.
Matt turned towards me and said, "Here we are, Deryk. This is Steyning. Do you want me to stay nearby or would you prefer it if I left you alone?"
I answered, "Thanks, Matt. I think I need to do this on my own."
I watched him wander away in the direction of the village.

I walked towards the old house; the front door was ajar. There was nobody around, so I took the chance to enter the hall, desperate to find John. A slight draught drifted through the doorway which caused the door to slam closed behind me.

I inhaled the sweet smell of smoked wood, the scent of the dark brown furniture displayed in the impressive stately hall. Someone was slowly walking down the winding stairs. The footsteps were coming closer. A wrinkled hand with very thin skin glided down the handrail, and when the staircase changed direction, an old man appeared holding a walking stick. He reached out his hand and I walked up the staircase to assist him.

"Good afternoon, sir." He smiled and shook my hand.

"Good afternoon to you, sir."

"Do you happen to be a little bit lost?"

"Please accept my apologies for entering your house without your permission. I just arrived by taxi to find John Launder's memorial, and I wonder whether you would be able to tell me where I can find it?"

"Oh, I see. Is that the reason for your visit? Of course I can. All you need to do is walk back through the same narrow road you came by, then from the Saxon Cottage you cross the main road, turn left, then carry on walking until you've passed the library. You will find John's memorial in a field opposite the museum."

"Thank you, sir, that's very kind of you."

"It's interesting you've come here to visit the John Launder memorial. Only a few people do, or they find his memorial by accident because they're visiting the museum. I hope you don't mind my asking you, but what's the reason you want to see his memorial?" The man scratched his chin.
"I've been doing some research for a study about martyrs in Sussex," I lied; "hence I came across John's name."
"Ah, I see. Well, some years ago, I was teaching history to a class in the old grammar school, just around the corner. We came to the story of John Launder, which caught the pupils' imaginations, not least because the final moments of his cruel story had taken place so close to the old room in which we were studying. The children were fascinated by the story. I assume you know this place is infamous for being the location of the horrendous event which took place on 23rd July 1555 when John Launder, a Protestant, refused to renounce his faith during the reign of Mary I, and was burned at the stake?"
I felt a lump in my throat. The last time ever I saw him was in Lewes, but tonight it was the first time I'd heard where and when John had died: a day after I had passed to the Otherworld. After my torture they took John away from the vaults below the sign of the Star Inn, brought him to Steyning, and he became the second martyr to have been executed miles away from his hometown.
A handsome young adult, with a life ahead of him, and

look what happened to him!
"I didn't know this was the exact location. I can imagine it caught the pupil's imagination because of the cruel history and I feel sorry for them, but I do appreciate your telling me what a horrendous thing happened here."
The man opened the door, gesturing to go outside, and we continued our walk towards the green.
"As the anniversary takes place on the last day of term in July, as a Protestant myself, we arranged an event to which we invited both Roman Catholic and Protestant members of Steyning to commemorate John's passing. Since that time, I've been marking the day every year by placing a black rose on the memorial."
I was mesmerised by the pretty landscaped green and was in deep thought about what the man had said. "That's a peculiar gesture. What persuaded you to place a black rose on John's memorial each year?"
There was no response. I turned to look at him and he seemed to have vanished, gone without a sound.

At the very same moment, I heard loud shrill calls coming from behind the trees. A flock of ravens appeared, gliding through the air with long wedge-shaped wings, and they landed on the small fence, their heads tilted, observing me with their mysterious black eyes. The wind started to pick up and at the same time, an immense dark cloud emerged in the sky casting a shadow over the green. The cawing ravens were flapping their wings, and their feathers released a grey powder. Large particles of dust were coming down, quickly falling out of the air, and it settled on the ground. The house too had turned grey, looking like an old-fashioned black-and-white photograph. I felt the dust sticking to my skin, on my face and my arms, and I noticed it was all over my clothes. I touched the dust with my fingers and sniffed it. It was ash, solid remains of fire, and it smelt of burned wood. Everything around me was covered in grey powdery dust and the air was filled with a familiar scent, a smoky open-fire scent. Memory and smell are intertwined, and my mind went back in time. I recognised it: it reminded me of that awful day. The crowds had gathered at the Star Inn, listening to what I had to tell them, everyone was surrounded by the same smoke. Just as I hoped, they had kept their word. Their descendants did not forsake my children, neither did they forsake my brewery and inn, instead the people of Brighton rebuilt The Black Lion, and nowadays it's a traditional pub carrying the same name and if people look up, they can see my weathervane from Flanders, showing them the direction of the wind. Ironically, the wind had stopped blowing through the green. I looked at the sky and saw the cloud moving eastwards, revealing a bright white moon standing above the horizon, and the ashes had stopped falling. Behind me I could hear footsteps, someone else had entered the green. I looked around but there was no one there. I was sure I heard the sound of steps through the grass, close to the house. Where had this person gone? Could it be the history teacher, who had tried to find his way back to the house? Should I say something, or should I keep my silence in case it was not the teacher but someone else? Then I remembered Matt's words 'You've got nothing to lose' and I realised he was right. I called out: 'Hello, anyone there?'

I could hear the footsteps again, and then a man emerged from behind the trees and walked towards me, keeping his head bowed. I have to admit he looked quite striking, wearing a dark green tunic, light brown trousers with a black belt tight around his slim waist and knee-high leather boots. His wide-brimmed black hat was tilted, concealing his eyes and most of his face, and I wondered who it could be? He stopped in the middle of the green and the moment he took off his hat, I recognised him.

"John, it is you, isn't it?"

I walked to him and embraced him, my arms holding him so tight, like it was the last time I was going to see him.

"Deryk, we finally meet again, I've been waiting so long for this moment to happen, I had almost given up hope, and accepted I would never ever see your face again," he said, crying tears of joy.

"I never knew this moment could happen, John. I can't believe I'm holding you in my arms again. It's been a hell

of a long time."
"We have been separated for such a long time, it felt like eternity, living in a realm where our spirits were sent to suffer for their sins."
"I deeply regret the moment I started talking to you in Godstone, engaging you in conversation and inviting you to come down to my brewery and inn, reading from my book. Look at what has become of us! Today, we meet again, on All Hallow's Eve, a day dedicated to remembering the dead and the anniversary of our arrest."
"There's no need to feel sorry, you're not the one to blame. It was the Heresy Act introduced by the Queen and Bishop Bonner who spoke the ultimate verdict. I guess we were in the wrong place at the wrong time. But, now we're here." John paused for a few seconds. "I need to tell you something, Deryk. When I watched you being burned, it was the most heartbreaking and painful thing to witness, and it left me in torment."
"John, I still feel guilty for what they've done to you."
"There was nothing you could have done to stop them. You were the first to die in Sussex, and moments after your death, Sheriff Edward Cage handcuffed me to him, and took me by horse and cart over the dry soil track roads to Steyning, a market town with a thriving and important port where ships would moor to alleviate the congestion at Portslade-by-Sea. I entered Steyning

through the town gate and arrived at a cobbled market square surrounded by half timbered white and black cottages where merchants sold wine, dried fruit, olive oil, spices and silver and iron. Towards the east stood a church with a tower built on a hill. The Sheriff took me to a house which was used as a prison. The following day, he walked me to the stake, which was positioned on a green opposite a timber framed building across from the church's garden, occupied by a chantry priest. When I approached the green, I was greeted by crowds of people. I looked as confident as ever with a proud smile on my face, just like you, I was ready to sacrifice my life. The Sheriff said to me, 'John, you've been a faithful man.' He knelt down, said his prayer, and asked me to strip off all of my clothes. Soon, I was standing naked in front of the men and women, and it looked like they felt sorry for me. Cage tied me to the stake, and lit the wood. Unlike you, I was not a man of many words, and I was looking at the crowds with an expression of pride on my face whilst the wood was crackling, and smoke and heat were rising from the logs. Within minutes, the orange flames were reaching higher and higher, getting close to my body. I couldn't hold it any longer, and screamed out loud. 'Have mercy upon me! I commend my spirit to rejoice in you, Deryk, wherever you are, step into my flame!' Those were my last words.'
Deryk gently kissed him.

"But, how ... ?" John asked him.
"Don't try to find the answer, this world we live in is just a place for the descended souls. We were sleeping, but now we are awake. Not far from here, deep in the dark, there's a coal black sea where the sky above the hills is on fire. It is as deep as the dreams of our desire and I would like to show it to you. Take my hand and walk with me. You're the one I love the most."

The End

Epilogue

Just before dusk, a man left his house to take his dog out for a walk, and crossed the road. It was quiet at this time of the evening, unlike the busy town where he used to live. The move from Sutton to Steyning had done him good; a lovely small market town with picturesque streets, and here he was part of a lively community of writers, artists and other creative people. He had heard tales of a spirit that haunted the village - some said it was the ghost of W.B. Yeats, a poet who used to live locally and his ghost had returned to Steyning to try to find his last mistress Edith who was at his bedside when he died. They walked past the Old Coach House approaching a hidden entrance tucked away behind it. In front of it stood a chalkboard pavement sign with the words 'Church Open' written on it. The man found it a bit odd that the church would be open at this time of the night and thought the Father might have forgotten to remove it. He walked over a winding path which led through a small tunnel of trees to the back of the St Andrew and St Cuthman Church, its ground covered with golden lights glowing in the dark. He had not seen this kind of light before, so he shook his head in disbelief, rubbed his eyes twice. He realised this was not a dream. Across the entire graveyard, he saw countless candles and lanterns and flowers placed on every single grave, remembering the dead who were buried here. His eyes studied the names on the headstones, there were so many of them. The man looked around him and took in the beauty of hundreds of flames blended with the fragrance of cinnamon, clove and oranges released by scented candles, lighting up even the darkest parts of this garden of the dead. He continued to walk over the winding path until he reached the front of the church. The wooden entrance door was open, which seemed to be a little bit strange at this time of the night, just like the pavement sign he saw earlier and he told his dog to wait at the entrance next to the bench. Eager to find out what was going on, he entered the nave which was filled with the intense earthy scent of frankincense, burning candles, and the smell of musty prayer books. The moonlight shone through the stained-glass windows, casting an eerie glow onto the dusty altar. Slowly he walked over the cold stone floor. His footsteps echoed in the nave, sending a flock of pigeons into disarray, cooing and flapping frighteningly away from the rafters. Situated between the large pillars stood a votive candle rack with small candles, lit by people to commemorate the spirits of the past, for the purpose of praying for the dead. Next to it stood a pretty little wooden table with a donations box, postcards and prayer books. The man's eye caught a pile of flyers and he picked one up. It explained the church had a fascinating collection of paintings and objects on display as part of an exhibition about the history of the bible and its impact upon the life of the nation for over two thousand years. So that was the reason the door had been left open, to invite people in and admire the collection the church had acquired. There was a range of colourful paintings displayed on its walls, and historical objects were placed on the tables in front of it. There was so much to see, but of particular interest was a preserved copy of a family bible published in 1550, originally belonging to a man named Deryk Carver, who lived in Brighton, and who had flung the book into the crowds before he was burned at the stake, becoming the first Lewes martyr. Someone had saved it and had handed it over to his family, who had passed it from one generation to another to preserve Carver's Bible, eventually ended up in a museum in Lewes. It was remarkable to see this book survived for so long, and it looked like it had received little damage over the years. There was merely a slight discolouration on some of the pages, but it looked as if there were blood stains on many pages, allegedly caused by the wounds that had been inflicted on the tortured soul. The man had read somewhere that dried blood stains could be used to bring a spirit back from the dead, but surely, no one would do such a thing these days, would they?

On this last day of October, once known as All Hallows' Eve, the time when walls between our world and the spirit world became thin enough to allow ghosts to pass through to the Otherworld, people lit candles on gravestones and left them burning all night in the darkness and solitude of the cemetery.

Like the others, he lit a candle, put a fifty pence coin in the collection box, left the church, and greeted his dog who had been waiting outside. Dry leaves were rustling in the wind as he walked through the wooden lychgate, set in a periphery flint stone wall, into Church Street. He was passing a little green, lit by an antique cast iron lamppost across the road, when the dog detected something. Dogs can tell from sniffing a tree or lamppost whether another dog has passed and who it is. Using their nose often seems to be the highlight of their walks. Tonight the dog took in and breathed out air in a very noisy way, which meant he had detected something major. The

dog trotted towards Chantry Green House, just when the deep and solemn sound of church bells started to ring, reminding the village to pray for the souls in purgatory.
In front of the house, someone had placed a group of little glass lanterns with burning candles. It reminded the man of what he saw earlier in the churchyard. Attracted by it, he moved closer and noticed the lanterns were placed in a circle around a patch of scorched soil, in the centre of which appeared to be the entwined smouldering bodies of two men, covered in a layer of fine ashes forming a protective shell around them. A light breeze made the lantern flames flicker and then the bodies disintegrated into fine sparkling particles, rising up into the night sky like embers.

As the man watched he saw the bonfires being lit on the surrounding hills, marking the beginning of long and dark nights of the autumn months, remembering the dead, stemming from an ancient belief that there is a powerful spiritual bond between those in heaven, and the living.

RBG

Website
www.richardbgough.com

Instagram
RichardBGough

Tumblr.
RichardBgough

Twitter
RichardBGough1

Richard's books are available from Amazon
and many other online retailers.

Martyrs Memorials in East Sussex

Brighton

Now built into the wall of the Black Lion on the corner of Black Lion Street with Black Lion Lane is a small tablet in memory of Deryk Carver, who was born in Dilsen-Stokkem, Luik/Liège, Belgium. Carver's home, once one of the oldest buildings in Brighton has now been re-constructed. The inscription on the memorial reads: 'Deryk Carver First Protestant Martyr burnt at Lewes July 22nd 1555, lived in this brewery'.

Directions: Black Lion, 14 Black Lion Street, Brighton BN1 1ND

Steyning

Designed and erected by the Sussex Martyrs Commemoration Council and unveiled 22 May 1997. John Launder (Godstone, Surrey) having been arrested in Deryk Carver's house in Brighton was brought here following his trial in London and condemnation on 10 June 1555. It is believed the stake was placed on Chantry Green close to the

Parish Church of St Andrew and St Cuthman. The memorial is to be seen close to the Library and the inscription reads: 'Near this spot on Chantry Green John Launder was burned at the stake 23rd July 1555 for refusing to renounce his Protestant beliefs during the reign of Queen Mary.

Directions: The Launder Memorial, Church Street, Steyning, BN44 3YB

Chichester

A memorial to Thomas Iveson (Godstone, Surrey) and Richard Hook (Alfriston, Sussex) was erected in 1948 and unveiled by the Hon. L. W. Joynson-Hicks, MP for the town.

Directions: The tablet is placed on the front façade of Providence Chapel in Chapel Street, Chichester, PO19 1BU

Lewes

A magnificent memorial stands on Cliffe Hill, Lewes and is visible from outside the Lewes Town Hall where the Martyrs were burned. The obelisk was erected in 1901 and was unveiled in 1905 by the Earl

of Portsmouth. The inscription on the memorial states that it was erected in loving memory of the seventeen martyrs (whose names are recorded) who for their faithful testimony to God's Truth were, during the reign of Queen Mary burned to death in front of the Star Inn, now the Town Hall, Lewes. In June 1949 a plaque was placed, by permission of the Town Council, on the façade of the Town Hall, over the vaults in which ten martyrs were imprisoned the night before their death. It states: "In the vaults beneath this building were imprisoned ten of the seventeen Protestant martyrs who were burned at the stake within a few yards of this site (1555-1557). Their names are recorded on the Memorial to be seen on Cliffe Hill. 'Faithful unto Death'
There is a small Tablet in the wall of Eastgate Baptist Church, Lewes placed by Mr Arthur Morris in Memory of the 17 Sussex Men and Women who died at the stake in Lewes during the reign of Queen Mary 1554-1557.

Directions: Cliffe Hill, Cuilfail Estate, Lewes BN7 2BE Access is through a private road, Cuilfail, belonging to Cuilfail Estate.

Source: sussexmartyrs.co.uk

Printed in Great Britain
by Amazon